Love Lost
to
The Solomon Sea

Love Lost to The Solomon Sea

by Naso Caleb Kila

Photo back cover: Michael Pennay Creative Commons license CC BY-SA3.0

Photo front cover: owner unknown

Published by Nenge Books, Australia, May 2025

ABN 26809396184

nengebooks1@gmail.com

www.nengebooks.com

ISBN 978-0-6459597-7-2

Love Lost
to
The Solomon Sea

A Novel

In memory of those lost at sea in
the MV Rabaul Queen Tragedy

by Naso Caleb Kila

Nenge Books

"I miss you in waves
and tonight, I'm drowning.
You left me fending for my life and
it feels like you're the only one who can
bring me back to the shore alive"

—Denice Envall

Dedication

To all the precious souls we lost on 02 February 2012, MV Rabaul Queen tragedy - a shipwreck that claimed more than 150 lives when it sank in the open Solomon Sea, near Finschhafen, Morobe Province, Papua New Guinea.

To my parents
Kila M Kasa & Tama K Isawana

Contents

Author's Note

This is a work of historical fiction inspired by true events. While certain events, locations, and timelines are based on historical records, the characters portrayed in this story, including their names, personalities, and dialogue are either products of the author's imagination or have been fictionalized for narrative purposes.

All names used in this story are fictitious. Any resemblance to actual persons, living or dead, is entirely coincidental and unintentional.

Preface

Have you ever heard the common phrase, "Life is unfair"?

I've heard it before, but I've always doubted it. Society has brainwashed me into believing and accepting that life is indeed unfair. You may have your perspective on it, but I choose to disagree.

Instead, I say, "Surely, we live in a cruel world where life is sometimes complicated and unpredictable."

Life breaks us to the point where we feel its deadly sting, yet we remain silent. Not because we cannot speak, but because the world we live in is so loud that it can't pause to listen to our painful and agonizing cries ringing from deep within our hearts.

In life, we experience highs and lows, battling through its raging storms. We pray and wish for another chance. We endure countless heartbreaks. We cry oceans of tears at night. We lose people we love. In the blink of an eye we lose everything we've built over the years. We make mistakes and, in doing so, lose those we once promised to spend forever with.

Life is full of unexpected goodbyes. The most painful goodbyes are often left unspoken - the ones that remain unheard by the person we long to reach.

And we wonder. What if they had heard us? What if we had heard them? No matter how badly we want to say something, sometimes, life never gives us the chance.

We are forced by the society we live in to accept that it was a goodbye after all. We carry within us the fear of that inevitable day, hoping to delay its arrival. But when the day finally comes, we have no control over it. We are left with no choice but to accept it, just as it is.

This is what happened in the early hours of February 2, 2012, when the MV Rabaul Queen sank. Many of us never had the chance to say our final goodbyes to our loved ones. And it hurts deeply to remember those who were lost to the sea in such an unimaginable, heartbreaking way. Their stories must be told.

)(

In this historical fiction story, I'll take you on a wonderful and interesting adventure of great love and loss. We're going to discover what Avundigi revealed after twelve years of self-isolation and loneliness after losing the love of his life on the MV Rabaul Queen.

Many stories of such unprecedented tragedy will never be told. Stories that left one to rest and the other with a broken heart, and the sun will surely set. The roses on a thousand hills will fade in their lives forever. But the kind of love that bound Avundigi and Michaellyn together seemed worth telling. It's the kind of Love that springs from deep within the heart and does not disappoint. A selfless love that is so pure, and you don't have to fight for it. It will always be yours.

It was True Love when an Eastern Highlander fell in love with the Morobean Princess. Unfortunately, it ended halfway, long before it even started. This will continue to hurt a little more until he knocks hard on heaven's door after nightfall.

"A love so cold as ice,
I don't want to let you go, honey
Not today, not in this way.
This must not be our sunset."

Introduction

As Avundigi stared intensely through the half-opened window one chilly morning at Kabiufa Adventist High School, his heart was captured at his first sight of Michaellyn. But little did he realise how tragically their love journey would end when the MV Rabaul Queen sank in the Vitiaz Strait near Finschhafen, off the northwest coast of Papua New Guinea.

Avundigi and Michaellyn were just high school students who became attracted to each other and agreed to turn their friendship into a sweet romantic relationship. Later, they discovered that they were more and more like each other. The way they talked about their dreams and future aspirations, in the way they communicated, did odd things, and had their being, all testified that they were born for each other by divine providence.

Their hearts were entwined, against the school rules, to beat in unison rhythmically under the misty mountains of Kabiufa. Their love story will not only bring tears to your eyes as you reach the final pages of this book, but will make you believe in a kind of love that was so down to earth. Love that was so kind, respectful, and didn't disappoint.

It is a love story that proves that true love exists in what we sometimes consider to be the broken pieces.

Their love story was a soft touch that went beyond the boundaries of love and true romance. Despite the challenges they faced in school; the time they had together; the distance that separated them years later after high school. They remained true to each other. Their bond remained strong due to the deep heart-to-heart connection they stitched together from first sight back in high school.

Their relationship was built on understanding, true love, and forgiveness, making their love even more sacred and romantic. The memories of their time together lasted longer than anyone could ever believe and wait for. Even years later, as Avundigi revisited the place where they first met and where they had been together, he felt like her presence was still there, like a gentle breeze. It was just like how the moon loved the lonely skies of the night so tenderly. How the lily loved the morning dew. Michaellyn was surely Avundigi's 'Almost home'.

"This is exactly where we met, right here on this spot," Avundigi whispered without looking at me, pointing towards where the water reservoir was. Tears formed in his eyes. When we came near the water reservoir after touring the majestic campus of Kabiufa Adventist Secondary School, he stopped, attempting to avoid a bleeding and shattered heart. He didn't want to go any further. For him, it was after so many years that he recollected withered memories, each step of the way.

"Just yesterday", Avundigi cried to himself as I watched eagerly. "Michaellyn came into my life and painted my soul with all the colors of the rainbows and beautiful vivid memories. In all the sunsets, and the blooming roses."

I never said a word. I stared at him respectfully, didn't know how to comfort him.

"Naso, she changed my life completely. I lost me, I don't know how to separate the past from the present now," he added as he bent over to grab a handful of dust and toss it into the air. I listened attentively with my arms folded and then placed them neatly behind my back. I zipped my mouth and watched him as tears started to fall like rain down my cheeks. At that point, I came to know that Avundigi and Michaellyn were more than true lovers, they were family.

PART ONE

Michaellyn

Chapter 2

Childhood and Separation

The best and sacred moment in the life of a parent is when they have time alone with their kids. Every child would testify that they loved the moments with their parents when they read them bedtime stories, played with them in the field and beach, or went for walks in the parks with them. When they grow older, they'll never forget all those memories buried in their hearts.

This was what happened in July 1990. A young couple, Denevi and Akaliah, with their two children, Jaybe and Michaellyn, walked barefoot along the Finschhafen Coast. That day will never fade from their hearts. It was a sacred moment of wonderful childhood memories. Akaliah ran around in a circle with 6-year-old Jaybe while Denevi playfully dug deep into the sand with Michaellyn before grabbing a handful of fine sand and tossing it into the air, letting it fall like rain.

When the sun slowly sets in the West, the day dies in the South Pacific. It has always been quiet and peaceful. The sun would freely rise to kiss the lonely Solomon Sea before it set. It would paint the waves and skies red like hot volcanic flames. Beholding the beauty of the waves on the Northeast Coast of Morobe, rising to move forward, backward, and in a continual set of motions, is one of the beautiful sights that excites those living along the coast. Finschhafen is one of the most beautiful places in the Pacific with its historical sites of World War II.

Michaellyn and Jaybe had their childhood in that beautiful and isolated part of the world. Many miles away from the street lights of Lae City. Their teen years were filled with joyous laughter. Michaellyn's gentle hands and smooth feet once collected weightless crystals of fine sand from the coast of Finschhafen. As she grew older, she left only the footprints behind. Like everyone else, Michaellyn and Jaybe grew beautiful and handsome, and enjoyed every moment of their life in a seaside village.

One evening, after the sun had set, the moon shamelessly forced itself out of the Bismarck Sea into the Pacific Skies. The heavens now had so many mountains of dark clouds. So dark that it hid the face of the October moonlight. The creeping insects and the hummingbirds sang their evening choruses harmoniously as they hurriedly made their way into the darkest soil and abandoned tree branches and holes.

Michaellyn heard the sound of the falling rain near Gagidu Primary School and ran against the buzzing wind into the kitchen with the bundles of broomsticks she had made from the dried leaves of the coconut tree.

"Michaellyn", Akaliah called while taking the clothes from the line outside. "You have already wasted so much time on this stuff! It has taken you almost an eternity to round it off. Can you please put that aside and help me peel the taro *kong kong* that is under the table? It's getting late, your father will be here at any moment."

"Yes, Mommy," she replied, carefully placing all the untied broomsticks behind the door. After spreading the old bag on the blind floor, she started peeling the taro *kong kong*. Just then, her father, Denevi, came in with a roll of fish. He was soaked from the rain.

"I felt for you when I saw the rain falling rapidly, without fear, like a rocket towards your direction," Michaellyn told her father who had just returned from the coastline fishing, as she hurriedly threw the peeled taro kong kong into the boiling water over an open fire.

Denevi left everything on the wooden table, hung his coat on the edge of the door, and sat around the fireplace to keep himself warm as the water kept dripping from his head into the fireplace. After he had changed himself into new clothes, he started telling Michaellyn what had happened when he was out at sea.

"Today, I went out with Jaro, an experienced skipper. He took the boat into the mountains of waves and crushed them. The waves were terrible. A messy day for both of us, we haven't caught enough".

"That's why you didn't bring so many fish, as you always do on weekends," Akalia interrupted while preparing the fish to boil in a pot of coconut cream.

After boiling the taro kong kong, Michaellyn continued with the broomsticks, dividing them into bundles and tying them firmly with tubes to sell them at the marketplace. While they were having dinner, the sky held back the rain, causing the mucky mud in front of the house to dry. The evening was quiet except for the evening bird songs. That's when Jaybee, a playful kid, came back home from playing with his friends in the rain on the other side of the road.

Michaellyn's grandma, Aiko, was old and full of years. She couldn't sit long enough around the fireplace, so she climbed onto her bed with no 'good night' before sleeping. Michaellyn, Jaybee, her parents, and her grandma lived a simple life in a countryside home far away from Lae City in Papua New Guinea.

Denevi is one of the great fathers. He was a Lutheran by faith, loving and protective of his young family. He always wanted the best for his wife and kids. Michaellyn, in her lifetime, never witnessed her father beating her mother at any time. He proposed in his heart not to plant the seed of fear in his children's hearts by arguing or fighting with his wife, Akaliah.

Michaellyn witnesses to how her father loved her mother. He was soft with a golden heart. He was kind, gentle, and loving towards his family. Denevi would bring gifts, even little gifts, for his wife and kids on their special days, like birthdays and Mother's Day, to appreciate them. A little reminder that he loved them still.

Michaellyn was different. She was quiet and would remain silent most of the time. She would allow her parents to talk when they conversed around the fireplace in the evenings. She was raised in a home filled with parental love, respect, and care. She never once said 'No' to her parent's instructions.

When given tasks like doing dishes, sweeping the house, doing her laundry, and helping her mother prepare dinner, she would do it efficiently and carefully. She was trained and taught to love what she was doing at a very young age. It was her influential mother, who was the best mother in the world to her kids and wife to her husband. Michaellyn grew up learning from her mother every day. Akaliah lovingly taught her everything a girl needs to do and learn. She could willingly do every chore in the house without even being told. Her mother played a vital role in her life; she didn't command her to do something, but helped her by guiding her with a low tone to do something.

One thing that motivated and inspired Michaellyn to love what she was doing, whether sweeping, cooking, doing her laundry, or to weeding in her garden, was when her parents appreciated and congratulated her for doing it perfectly, even if there's some dirt on the collar of her shirt she washed or some weeds she missed uprooting in the garden.

The appreciation from her parents boosted her self-esteem and confidence to do better with a second chance. Her parents saw positive changes in her life as she grew older. She loved greeting people with gentle smiles, warm hugs, and sharing what she has with them, whether food or whatever she has. From all the great traits Devevi and Akaliah noticed in their daughter Michaellyn, what troubled them most was her ability to be alone. She would be out in the garden weeding or transplanting for hours, with all her mind and heart in whatever she was doing. She was the invisible member of the family.

A year before she went to school, Denevi bought her paints and a brush to develop her finger muscles to hold the pencil. He also brought her Uncle Arthur's bedtime story books, which later became her favorite book collection to read at school. She would read for hours and hours without getting tired or exhausted. She loved reading. She would paint anything: mountains, plants, rivers, the rising and the setting of the sun on the surface of the sea. Michaellyn loved to paint flowers she found around the house and would paint them artistically. She had a wonderful childhood.

February 1994

In 1994, she started attending Gagidu Primary School. Devevi would read her bedtime stories from her reading books. One thing she was told to do when things went wrong was to make 'Restitution'. It happened because when one of her classmates was having lunch at school, and Michaellyn accidentally bumped into her, causing her piece of sweet potato to fall on the ground. She then apologetically offered her lunch and went home hungry. At school, Michaellyn was told to respect her teachers and other students, and obey school rules at all times.

Her first-grade teacher, Ms. Wilson loved Michaellyn so much and encouraged her to keep reading and memorizing her 12 times tables. She had this attitude of being alone in the crowd most of the time. She didn't have many friends with whom she could open up for conversations, so the only place she found peace of mind was in the books she read.

One day, Michaellyn came back from school and found that Denevi had become very ill during the day. She attentively stood by her mother's side to hear what she would say to help him get back to health. As the night approached, his body became very hot, and the sickness grew worse. He couldn't walk. His legs were paralyzed. He was unable to lift his foot. Michaellyn helped him into the kitchen and seated him close to the fireplace, where he would be kept warm through the night.

A cup of tea was brought to him, which he drank in silence. His mind was troubled. He felt a deep pain in his back and right foot. Every night when everyone went to bed, Michaellyn would stay up late beside him. Listening to the echoes of her father's agonizing pain in his back, till her eyes would turn red, and then she would go to bed. The love between a daughter and a father cannot be broken by time and long distance.

For the next few days, she was absent from class. She wanted to stay home and take care of her father. The illness lasted longer that they had anticipated, and he was diagnosed with bone cancer in the femur and the spinal cord. By then, he was crippled and bedridden. Denevi had been sick for years, but all this time, he had hidden the pain just for his children. Now, the sky has turned to grey, he couldn't hide anymore.

One day Michaellyn came home, and her father wasn't there. He was dragged outside the house, and seated under the shade. Michaellyn came and sat close to him. She told him everything that happened at school, she told him of how she answered most of the questions asked in class, and showed him her test papers. Denevi was pleased.

"Michaellyn, you're so young and have so many years to live on. As your father, I would hate to see young girls being mistreated, abused, and becoming single mothers just because they are uneducated. Education is life, and it is the only tool you'll use to eradicate poverty in your life, community, and the country," Denevi told Michaellyn. She was too young to take to heart what seemed like her father's last words.

Devevi, realizing that Michaellyn had missed a lot of classes lately, urged Michaellyn to go to school. Michaellyn would wake up early in the morning to make her lunch, place it nicely into her string bilum, and always make a cup of tea for her father before she rushed off to school. For Denevi, instead of getting better, the illness grew worse, and he couldn't lift a foot or walk.

Every day, Michaellyn would run back home to care for her father and do everything he instructed from his bed or wherever he was. Aiko suspected that it was sorcery-related and tried to bring people who could perform traditional magic methods of healing, but Denevi turned the idea down because of his Christian faith and beliefs.

Denevi intuitively knew that his medical trip to Lae would end in disaster. He knew he would be overtaken by cancer, coupled with deep sorrow and loneliness over his young family. He knew that if only Akaliah took Michaellyn back to Markham, her grandparents would help to provide for her and lovingly raise her.

Denevi was on a boat to Lae the next day. In the days that followed, the sickness grew worse, and he couldn't fight any longer. Angau Memorial Hospital walls can attest that he had tried his best. Sadly, he was overtaken in the middle of the night a few weeks after he arrived.

When Michaellyn woke up, she didn't know that the final goodnight last night was her last goodbye. Michaellyn, in between her tears shed for her father, asked if she would be allowed to see his face, just his face. But she was not given a chance to see her father's face. At the dawn of a new day, all their neighbors came for the funeral, and her life has never been the same since then.

She was introduced to a world she didn't recognize anymore. It was too early to be called fatherless. The kind of separation when a father dies, and a mother from a faraway land would be found hopeless and helpless, with no power to fight for what her husband has left behind, with her kids being taken away from her. After the burial, Jaybee was taken away by his father's elder brother, Job. A respected person in the community. Akaliah was left alone with Michaellyn, because she was a girl.

A month later, Akaliah felt the unbearable pain of being a single mother. Her heart was temporarily stitched just to stop the bleeding. She didn't have enough money to support her children, especially Michaellyn. She was hit by poverty and had no hope. She would have committed suicide if it weren't for Michaellyn. She must have prayed in her heart to carry the burden upon her shoulders. She proved the fact that mothers will give up their lives for their children. She decided to take the risk for the sake of Michaellyn. She made up her mind to return back to her place in Markham.

They had a party and farewelled Akaliah and Michaellyn. Akaliah promised Jaybee and other members of Job's family that Michaellyn would return when she grew older to see her father's graveyard. That was the last time Michaellyn saw her brother Jaybee, who held Michaellyn in his arms, and they wept loudly. Everyone who was there had their rainfall of tears to shed.

Chapter 3

Emotional Journey to Lae

The night was young and very quiet. The moon, the stars, and the heavenly luminous bodies failed to shine their light on the earth that night. The darkness was still silky and deafening. You couldn't hear yourself or random whispers. Akaliah woke up and sat quietly on the bed, staring at the blind walls, hoping and praying for daybreak as the final hours to leave Finschhafen and return to Markham approached at the speed of light at early dawn.

She reached out for the torch near her pillows and went out of the house, washed her sleepy face with the bucket of water near the door, and walked around the overgrown lawn, thinking about Denevi and the trip that was ahead of her. She was filled with deep sorrow as thoughts of what the future held blinded her soul. She went back into the kitchen and lit the fire. That was the last time she'd keep herself warm from the fireplace where she had promised to live happily ever after.

When the flames were ablaze, she could now see Michaellyn resting peacefully on her mat. She quickly packed a few of her chosen clothes, many of which had been prepared the day before, and packed for Michaellyn in a separate bag, enough for her to carry when she woke up. At around 5:30 am, Michaellyn woke up from a deep sleep. It came to her memory what her mother had told her earlier, that today they would leave Finschhafen and go to Lae.

Her tears must have fallen, only the heavens might have counted them. At dawn, they carried their bags and hurried to the Finschhafen District Office and went down to the main wharf where the boat was waiting for them. Aiko and other families were waving as the boat slowly made its way out to sea. Michaellyn held on so tightly to her mother as the boat rocked back and forth against the waves from Finschhafen to Lae.

When they arrived at Lae Wharf, they were picked up by her uncle David, who was there waiting for them, and they drove straight to Chinatown, where he bought them lunch. Michaellyn was already starving to death, for they had eaten nothing since morning when they left Finschhafen. She never said anything, just a word of gratitude to her uncle David as she enjoyed the best chicken, which she confessed she hadn't had in a long time. From there, they took the back road to Tent City, where he resides.

Michaellyn couldn't comprehend how her mother must have felt that night as she fought unknown battles in her mind, staying up till late at night. Akaliah was a most beautiful young woman in her 30s. She had long, black curly hair, which she usually tied in two rows behind her back. Her life was turned black in a very unbearable way. Akaliah never knew of the pain of being a single mother that was awaiting her. Michaellyn, in her innocence, never knew life would be this harsh, this much pain that is waiting for her. They only realized it when the waves of reality swept across their face.

On Monday of the following week, David took Michaellyn and her mother to Markham. They left the city before 10 am and arrived three hours later at Umi, Markham Valley. Akaliah and David were welcomed by her grandparents, Bubu Auvo and Bubu Mama, and other extended family members who had heard of what happened to Denevi. Many came and shed tears as they had never been to Denevi's funeral, though they'd heard of what happened to him. Michaellyn felt accepted and welcomed in her mother's place. She quickly made friends with the village girls of her age and would do things freely on her own.

Michaellyn stayed with her grandparents when Akaliah went down to Lae City looking for opportunities and found a cleaning job with Lae Biscuit Company. While Akaliah was away, Michaellyn was bullied by her cousins in the village because Bubu Mama treated her in a very special way. Akaliah's heart was torn into pieces when Michaellyn reported the matter to her about what happened when she was away, but she couldn't do anything. Over the Christmas period, Akaliah talked to David concerning Michaellyn, and the following year, she went down to Lae, where she would go to school with her cousins.

February 1998

David enrolled Michaellyn at Lae Adventist Primary School, along with her cousins, Jerome and Laelyn. Michaellyn and Laelyn enrolled in grade three and they shared the same table. Life without her mother was like a separation that could never be reunited. Akaliah was with Michaellyn in Lae for a while before she left Lae Biscuit Company and went back to Markham, but would visit Michaellyn from time to time. She was picking up from where her husband had left to raise her only daughter by selling coconuts, peanuts, and fried chicken at Umi Market, along the Highlands Highway.

Michaellyn loved to go to school with her cousins and enjoyed all the class activities together. Lulume loved Michaellyn very much as her child. But as time went by and when she realized that David was giving most of his attention to Michaellyn, she started treating Michaellyn very poorly, accusing her of little things she did wrong at home. This went on for a while. Over time, such unkind and harsh treatment changed the course of Michaellyn's life forever. She became a lonely girl with poor self-esteem, losing her voice, self-worth, and feelings of belonging. She was a bright student but her marks dropped academically and she became an average student in class.

She would sit and watch other students play and have fun around the school campus. No one turned up to be her friend, not because she was ugly, but because she was invisible. She was alone in a crowd and would run away and find solace in a world of books. Her favorite collection of books was Uncle Arthur's Bedtime Stories.

She would read it word by word every night before bed. Sometimes, Lulume would send Michaellyn to school without lunch. Instead of lunch, she trained her stomach to have lunch of books to nourish the brain, instead of food for the body. She would sit under the tree and read as many pages as she could before the bell rang to signal the students that lunch was over.

Over time, those books inspired her and she decided to be a teacher one day so that she could help other students. Especially those like herself, the unfortunate ones who got camouflaged with the others in the school and were not recognized. Her prayers were so silent that the walls and ceiling in the house couldn't hear it. The desks she rested her head on in hunger could not hear her cry for it was without tears.

A strange and terrible feeling captured her soul, and she bowed her head low to find answers to where life was taking her. Her story was a very complicated puzzle. One thing that was so unique about Michaellyn was that she never mentioned any of the bad, harsh, and ugly treatment she got from her uncle's wife, Lulume, to David or anyone else. The only person she reported to was her mother, but what would she do? Absolutely nothing. She couldn't argue with Lulume or David.

David finally discovered what Lulume secretly did to Michaellyn, and his heart was gracefully broken. He loved Michaellyn just as he loved his children, and he was troubled. He talked about it to Lulume, but by then it was too late; Michaellyn had her heart hardened and vulnerable to change. Her uncle had raised Michaellyn for the past five years and treated her like his own child until she went to Eastern Highlands Province.

Chapter 4

Lonely Hill — Eastern Highlands

On 17 February 2003, a White Land Cruiser travelled up the Okuk Highlands Highway during the intense heat of the day. The truck carried only three people: Akaliah, Michaellyn, and Lulume. They arrived in the little town of Goroka, in the Eastern Highlands Province at midday. After refuelling, they had their lunch at Papindo Kai Bar, before they left Goroka Town and travelled the potholed road toward the East. As they got closer and closer to Lahame, the air grew thinner and warmer. They drove through the sun-scorched mountains of Upper Bena, and up the lowly hills until they arrived at a primary school situated peacefully on a mountain top. The school signboard at the gate read;

"Welcome to Bena Top Up Adventist
Primary School"

Motto: "Nothing Without Work"

As they jumped off the truck and looked around the beautiful campus, Ms. Phineas, a young female teacher, approached and welcomed them to the school. It was indeed a beautiful place, surrounded by eucalyptus and pine trees hanging on a hill overlooking Mount Michael in Lufa District, Daulo Pass, and the Ungai Ranges. At the foot of the hill flows the crystal-clear river that turns milky when it rains.

Michaellyn finally got herself registered as a boarding student. As the sun painted the sky red and evening approached, Akaliah held Michaellyn tightly, and they wept openly on a hill. Little did Michaellyn know that the very hill where she stood with her mother was called 'Lonely Hill'. The hill that collected the last tears that fell.

She stood there, lost in the buzzing wind, watching as the white truck disappeared down the slopes and hid in a cloud of dust. The pain of loneliness which thrust into her soul was unbearable. That day, Michaellyn returned to the dormitory, trying to suppress the emptiness by falling into a deep sleep, but her thoughts drifted back to her mother, and she couldn't go to sleep easily.

Very early in the morning, the school bell rang for two minutes, 30 dongs. She woke up along with the other girls and got ready to begin the new school year. The school rules were very strict. They had two meals a day: brunch at 10 a.m. and dinner at 6 p.m. Classes ran from 8 a.m. to 3 p.m., followed by a two-hour workline period before the evening program, which included worship and night study. That was how the school was run daily.

During the school principal's welcome speech, students, mostly primary-aged, were reminded that they were not in a holiday camp and were expected to study, work, and follow the rules.

"If you don't work, you simply don't eat," he told them.

That was a simple instruction. But to Michaellyn, it was a battle she had to fight. Weekends were for doing laundry down at the river. Any student who broke the rules was punished by carrying stones from the river uphill. It was a harsh but effective discipline method, regardless of your age. A punishment nobody wants to experience.

Michaellyn found it difficult to fit in with the other girls. She preferred to be alone most of the time, as she always had in the past. When someone greeted her, she would just smile. Life on the hill was peaceful and enjoyable. She would wake up in the morning, go for morning devotions, then to class, brunch, and soon after class. They were required to work for two hours, before they got ready for evening devotion and study. She was preoccupied so she didn't have time to waste and worry. She wasn't the only student from far away, there were many other students from all over the eight districts of Eastern Highlands Province.

One day, she was punished for being absent from the work line and evening worship. Her punishment was to carry fifteen stones from the river to the school ground. Those stones would be used to build flower beds and footpaths. (Those very stones remain there to this day.) After carrying ten stones, she was tired and exhausted. They were big stones. Two girls, Stephanie and Hannah, were down at the river doing their laundry when they noticed Michaellyn coming to and from to carry the stones. They knew what it felt like to be punished, so they decided to help her. When she returned to the river to collect some more, they called out to her.

"Hello, come here, we'll help you," Hannah told her.

They also gave her some biscuits to regain her strength, and as they ate together, they introduced themselves. Hannah was from East Okapa, and

Stephanie was from Henagaru, in West Okapa. Michaellyn didn't know where those places were. She just nodded. As they returned from the river, Stephanie pointed towards Okapa and showed Michaellyn where their place was.

"In life, we don't meet people by accident,"
Michaellyn would later reflect.

"Some come to teach us, guide us, motivate us, or even break us.

Every encounter has a purpose"

Michaellyn was liberated from her punishment by Stephanie and Hannah. They soon became close friends with Michaellyn. They would help each other with everything they needed. They would tell her a lot about their ples, culture, staple foods, and many other things. Michaellyn kept everything secret, except for telling them that she came from Morobe Province.

Despite the mutual friendship they developed, Michaellyn still felt lost. She was haunted by a question, "Where do I go from here?" She wanted to go to high school but had no idea where to. One day, everything changed during a rainy brunch break when her mathematics teacher, Ms. Phineas, walked into the classroom. Half of the students were outside, but Michaellyn remained inside with her head buried under her desk. She was reading.

Ms. Phineas approached her gently and asked, "Hello, are you okay? Why don't you come with me for lunch?"

Michaellyn looked up and was a bit surprised. She hesitated but followed Ms. Phineas. They walked past the school administration building to her house behind the chapel. Ms Phineas offered tea and buttered biscuits to Michaellyn. As they began to chat, Ms. Phineas shared her experiences at Kabiufa Adventist High School. She spoke about its friendly atmosphere, the well-maintained campus, the dedicated teachers, the students, and the spiritual programs. Michaellyn listened intently. For the first time, someone truly believed in her. Someone saw her potential.

"Ms Phineas, do you think I can make it to Kabiufa High School?" Michaellyn asked hesitantly.

"Honey, you can go anywhere in the world. Nothing can stop you if you have the drive and determination to chase your dreams," Ms. Phineas replied with a smile. From that day on, Ms. Phineas and Michaellyn became very close friends. Ms. Phineas had finally found the student she had been looking for, and Michaellyn had finally found someone who inspired her as well.

After Michaellyn was punished, she became one of the bravest and most faithful students. She had lots of friends, including teachers. She had a lot of experiences during the time she was there, including those moments she would walk down to the farm, and tearful evenings wasted on the Lonely Hill. She performed extremely well and scored good marks on her report card.

The school year ended with tears, memories, and of course, unspeakable joy. Saying goodbye to Stephanie, Hannah, and Ms. Phineas was one of the painful things she was forced to do. They weren't sure if they would ever meet again. At the school gate, they hugged, shedding warm tears as they departed. Michaellyn was picked up by the same white Land Cruiser that had brought her there.

As she left, the only memories that remained were scattered like specks of dust on the Lonely Hill.

On February 27, 2004, the day before leaving for Kabiufa High School, Akaliah travelled from Markham to Lae to accompany Michaellyn to school. There were many students from Morobe travelling to Kabiufa High School on that day. Akaliah and Michaellyn took the first bus to Goroka, arriving at Kabiufa Adventist High School at noon.

Unlike Bena Top Up Primary School, Kabiufa was much colder, located 10 km north of Goroka Town. It has a beautiful campus with well-kept lawns, beautiful flower beds, and numerous buildings. As they walked around, she learned about the school's history. The locals were friendly and accommodating. Teachers and students dressed neatly. They were disciplined. The school was a community of its own. Everything Ms. Phineas had told her was true, it had not been a fairytale. Michaellyn registered as a boarding student.

PART TWO

Avundigi

Chapter 5

Love at First Sight

March 2004.

The caretakers expertly mowed the lawn over the Christmas Holiday in preparation for the new school year. New shoots of grass responded to the dewy night showers and sprouted out, beautifying the field between the junior block and the teacher's residences.

I rested my head against the cold brick walls in one of those classrooms connected to the home economics building, whose windows were half opened towards the immaculate lawn. The same footpath led to the dining hall, chapel, girl's dormitory, and classrooms.

We had just completed the registration, and I was worried, trying to unfold the complicated and puzzling thoughts of home in my mind before heading to the dining hall for dinner. The classroom walls felt cold as I stared out the window, watching students approach the dining hall from every direction. If this had been a dream, I would have awoken, but this was reality.

I saw a very beautiful girl, the girl in dreams, walking towards the dining hall with her hands neatly folded behind her back. I was curious and tried to see clearly, but the louvers were blurry, and I couldn't. I had to wait till she came closer. Her curly hair was combed and tied into two rows behind her head. She walked in the middle, separate from the group of girls ahead and behind her. I was eager to know more, but I couldn't.

She seemed determined and focused. Even from where I was, I could tell she was happy. She had a medium green plate with a rainbow stripe outside and a reading book in her hand, which she hid with her plate so that nobody could tell she had a book. But as she came closer to the window, I could tell. The golden rays of the evening sun that shone through the leaves of the large eucalyptus next to the chapel shone on her hair, making it look like paradise in the green valley of Kabiufa.

When she turned towards the window, suspecting that someone was staring at her, I looked away and immediately walked out of the classroom from fear and embarrassment, carrying only her facial image in my mind. There were many students when I walked into the dining hall and stood in front of the middle door. Within a second, my eyes had scanned all the corners of the noisy building, before I sat down on one of the seats near the door, leaning against the brick wall waiting for the food to be served.

That evening, the dinner would be rice and cabbage with fish. While someone was serving, I bowed my head low, resting my face against the table, trying to recall what I had seen earlier, before it would completely disappear from my memory. All I could remember was the color of her hair and a few facial features, her left eye, ear, and hand. Just like Nokondi of Eastern Highlands, only one side of her body became visible in my mind.

When the bell rang for the second time for evening worship, everyone vacated the building, leaving me alone, barely able to lift a foot.

"Avu, she's just a random girl, a bird flying above your imagination. Let it go," I whispered to the empty tables and chairs before running back to the dormitory.

By the time I arrived, everyone was already dressed in suits and ties for the evening worship.

I quickly changed into my long trousers and blue shirt, then joined the others, who were already singing melodiously in the chapel. Mentally, I stood at a crossroads.

"Should I let her go or hold on to the hope that I would see her again?"

I believe there were unlimited possibilities.

I was distracted throughout the program led by the senior students. Falling in love was against school rules, and I never intended to do so, but I couldn't erase the picture of that girl in my mind. I knew the risks involved, yet I couldn't help but house the thought carefully, sacredly in the depths of my soul. In fact, it was not love that I craved, it was totally something else, a sacred admiration I have for someone I knew I would love to keep forever.

I only realized the service had ended when everyone stood up to sing the closing hymn, "I Serve a Risen Savior", from the Adventist Hymnal. As they offered the final prayer, I hurried outside, walking quickly toward the dormitory.

"She's not just a girl," I assured myself. "She was tall, fairly dark, and had an appealing beauty, like the wild orchids I've seen in the tropical forests back in Okapa. I must find her".

With that thought hibernating in my mind, I hit the dormitory wall and went to bed, but my heart was at war with my mind, and I was greatly disturbed. These twists and turns were so disturbing to my cube mates. I stood up, walked outside the dormitory and around the field before I returned, and this time, I was off to the land of dreams.

For the next few days I felt like I was in a coma, mentally infected by her smile and diagnosed with a broken heart. I admired the way she walked; it was as if she was kissing the earth with her feet. I was a shy person. I never opened up to conversations with anyone. I always kept it to myself, and so if I ever happened to cross paths with her, making the first move, for me, would feel like a horrible suicide.

I never knew her name, where she came from, which primary school she attended, and what grade she's in now; the only thing I knew was that she resides within the school premises, which gave me a little hope to hold on to the idea that I'll see her again.

I couldn't recall what day, but I'm pretty sure it must be on Wednesday evening, right after dinner. I decided to wash the dishes, so I grabbed the dish on which our dinner had been served and walked outside towards the water tank near the chapel. On arrival, there were many students already there. Disappointed, I sat on the concrete slab that was there, my back facing the kitchen. Behind me, I could hear some girls walking towards me, giggling with laughter. They passed me by and headed towards the tank, but there was this kind soul who saw me with the dish and turned back to help me.

"Hello, are you alright? Let me help you wash the dishes," she asked.

"Oh really, great, thanks, Miss. So kind of you," I exclaimed!

"You're welcome, I'm Michaellyn,"she replied.

"I'm Avundigi".

"Nice to meet you, Avu, I mean Avundigi, please forgive me," she smiled.

She was the girl I've been dreaming of for the past few days. I would be committing a horrible sin if I said it was a divine intervention. But if it was, then I was innocent. I tried to catch my breath but failed. I kept looking at her, and she excused herself and turned toward the water tank.

I felt as if she had taken something away from me. Not just my sinking heart, but my soul, and everything that made me into a living being. I tried to resist looking in her direction, but I couldn't. I had sinned. I knew she was not an ordinary girl. I wasn't falling in love with her instantly. It wasn't love. It was something else, something deeper, a sacred admiration.

I stood up and slowly walked away. After that incident, I crossed paths with her on several occasions, but not too close for a hello.

Until one day, I was sitting when she came alone under the tree near the administration building.

"Hey, hello. Avundigi, right?" Michaellyn called softly from behind.

"Yes, that's correct," I answered, trying to recall her name. She noticed the confusion on my face and saved me from my struggle to remember.

"I'm Michaellyn. Would you mind if I sit here?" she asked politely.

"No, not at all," I replied, and she sat just a meter away on the same bench.

We were close, very close, yet after that brief exchange, silence crept in between us. The wind blew, the leaves fell helplessly to the earth, and very few students climbed the stairs to the administration building. Some wandered across campus, scattered in different directions. And yet, under the rain tree, breathing the same air, sharing the same table, we sat without a word. Then something struck me, I had never properly introduced myself. Why should I? I should have said something. This time, I decided to let her take the lead. I could tell she was a Morobean, but I never asked.

It was a long weekend, and many students had gone home. The campus was growing emptier and quieter. The evening turned dull as dark clouds loomed overhead. I watched as she stood up and slowly walked back to the dormitory. I had missed my chance.

I felt guilty. I hated myself for not having the courage to speak up. Just a conversation with a girl. If there was one girl in the entire world that I truly loved and admired, it would definitely be Michaellyn. This feeling hadn't come out of nowhere; it had grown, slowly taking root in my heart with each brief encounter, every exchanged smile on campus. It was an irresistible, rare feeling, one I couldn't escape, no matter how hard I tried.

But I had to fight through it. I couldn't just run up to her and hug her on her way to class or while she carried her spade, heading to the farm. Even if such things were allowed, I would have been seen as a fool for doing them.

What drew me closer to her day by day was her sense of responsibility. She walked around on campus with purpose and responded positively to everything around her. She had my full attention at school. She was my difficult subject in class. I admired the way she picked up stray papers from the campus lawn, gathered empty plastic bottles on her way to class, and dressed neatly, her hair carefully done on Saturdays. I was her silent admirer. Time passed, and I never found the right moment to confess what was in my heart. Then, the school closed for the first-term break.

When we returned for the second term, I discovered that she had never left. She had stayed on campus throughout the holiday. Questions filled my mind. I wanted to understand her better. Why didn't she go home for the term break? She seemed to have many friends, yet she was often alone, reading her Bible in an empty church, buried in books in a deserted classroom, or sitting under a tree, lost in her thoughts. She always recognized me when we crossed paths, and we exchanged soft, fleeting smiles. But I knew those smiles were not real. They were not something I could hold on to. I couldn't trust those smiles to hope for something more. I never tried to make a fool of myself crossing her line, so I kept my distance.

One day she was absent from class, the dining hall felt empty without her smile, church programs became boring, and the work line wasn't effective as it used to be. I was worried as if we were close friends. How did I know that she was absent? I never found her. When I asked one of her classmates, she told me that she had become ill and was in the dormitory.

On Friday of that week, she turned up for breakfast, and I could tell that it was not the sickness that made her ill; she was depressed, she was lonely. She was often found alone in the crowd of students; she lived in a world of loneliness and isolation. She had more than what I could comprehend from afar. A few days later, I saw her with a woman standing in front of the canteen, chatting without looking at each other. The woman brought her something, and she was trying to unpack the goods from the plastic.

There were visitors, students, and teachers going in and out of the gate, and there were two, a mother figure and a pious daughter, cherishing the moment they had, knowing that it would be the only one for the next couple of months. I guess her mother must have come to see Michaellyn after hearing that she was sick. The bond of love shared between a mother and her daughter is something my little mind couldn't comprehend, where they could read the silence, and not a word was needed for further explanation.

When the bell rang for the work line, they walked towards the main road to the bus stop where her mother was picked up by the PMV bus to town, and Michaellyn returned back to the dormitory. These were the few moments that caught my attention to truly confess that Michaellyn is not just an ordinary girl, she is one of a kind. We don't often find such birds dominating our skies today. Every time when I saw her, anywhere on the campus, I felt like we had something in common.

I do not know what exactly it was, but I do believe she does so as I do. It never came to mind what date it happened, but as I recollected those memories from my diary, it was on Thursday. I was with my workmates coming back from the farm after the work line. When we reached the greenhouse, my very best friend, George, from Kainantu, when trying to slice the wild grass by the roadside, landed the sharp edge of his grass knife on my ankle, which bled vigorously. Since my blood was circulating actively in my body, it spilled out, and I almost fainted and was rushed to the water reservoir next to the boy's dormitory. George then cut the edge of his shirt and tied it around the wound just to stop the bleeding. After everyone left, George and I sat back on the bank waiting for the pain to ease so I could go to the dormitory.

Coming my way from the farm were many girls, among them was Michaellyn. She noticed that my left foot had been tied, and she came over, trying to investigate what had happened to me. At closer look, she realized that I had been wounded, and tied with the old cloth, so she offered me a new band-aid and asked if she could bandage my sore properly, which I agreed and she nursed it very well.

"Ah, Michaellyn, I'd be glad if you became a nurse," I joked in complimenting her job well done.

"Stop it, Avundigi, I hate medicine and hospitals and all that stuff," she replied as she gave me the best smile she had reserved for many years.

I told her what happened and how I got injured. She was very sorry, but I assured her not to worry as it would heal very soon. George was on the other side of the lake, feeding the fish with the bread crumbs he collected from the bin earlier.

We sat there as the last rays of the setting sun set over the mountains of Daulo Pass. She ignited the conversation that would lead to a beautiful love story, and yet, I was unprepared for it.

She was very beautiful; she had no dimples except a cute curve on her cheeks when she smiled, and eyes looked like the eyes of an eagle when she half-closed them. Her long curly hair was tied in two rows behind her back. I felt no pain in my ankle anymore. She was friendly, and I never jump to conclusions!

This is where she told me a little bit about herself upon my request, and I did the same. In between her words, she never mentioned her father, she only introduced her mother to me by the mention of her name, Akaliah. When the bell rang for the evening program, I turned right, she turned left, and our eyes were crushed; if someone had been there, they could have seen the sparkles of love falling in between us like leaves during winter.

She knew I loved her, and I knew she would be the same if I took the plunge and ask her out. But I didn't. As we said goodbye, she asked if we could meet again on Friday, and I agreed before we dispersed to our respective dormitories. As George and I walked down to the dormitory, George was smiling and laughing at the same time.

"Bro, she loves you," he told me. I just don't want

you to talk about her, I thought. I quickly turned his idea down and changed the subject before he ruined it!

"She is the girl I've been dreaming of, it's no longer a dream, the virtual in my mind has finally become my reality," I whispered to the walls that had heard my midnight wishes for so long, as I rested my head against the wall and went to bed. I closed my eyes, but my mind was awake the whole night, dragging me back to where I first saw Michaellyn, as if it were just yesterday. It's a mystery. Why would I get attached to someone who speaks a different language, someone I never knew before? Why would I fall in love with her so easily? It appeared to me as a wonderfully complicated mystery.

We met again on Friday, and it was a real romance without roses. I didn't know how it felt until she came alone and she jokingly hit me and I never felt any pain, then I knew I fell deeply in love with Michaellyn, a love that does not disappoint either. There were not so many students on campus that day, and we were distracted by no one. We playfully walked down to the pool where she had met me previously, and there, after we watched the school of fish, I blindly confessed my raw feeling that I loved her.

"I love you too, Avu," she replied. We didn't know how long it would go, but we decided to take the risk, or loss it all, if not, for the rest of our lives.

She accepted me just as I was, and I loved her just as she was. And it makes the difference I wouldn't have seen and experienced if I hadn't walked down that road. She tells me everything, there's nothing that she has kept from me. When she mentioned her late father, I felt for her, seeing how she was so courageous to be brave and strong to fight against the tides of life. The day ended with us throwing pebbles and bread crumbs into the pool and watching the school of fish fighting against each other over a piece of bread. In between us, there was nothing, precisely nothing, except rain of pure love falling daily, heavily.

Before I met Michaellyn, I was a bad boy, a complicated teenager. I had a terrible childhood in a remote part of Okapa in Eastern Highlands Province. I never said I have a cruel family, no, my father was a loving and kind person. My mother wears a smile wherever she goes. I was blessed with a loving family. I was born after my elder brother. We were five in a family. The problem with second-born children is being bossy and disobedient sometimes, and by all means, I fall into this category.

But it all changed because of Michaellyn, who spoke no word, just genuine love and kindness. I changed just to love and to protect her. How can I hurt someone who loved me like how the moon loves the night? For the next couple of months, we got to know each other, our likes and dislikes, our favorite foods, and places of dreams, the type of color we admire and where we want to spend our free time. She was not event-oriented, nor was I. She loves simple street food, as do I. She loves hiking and visiting places. We had uniform hearts.

She preferred books and quiet places. She had a deep connection with the nature of books. She would spend hours reading and reading and reading. Sometimes when we were together, she would forget that I was there if she had a book in her hand.

Often, I jokingly teased her, saying; "Mickey, I will not be surprised to find you falling in love with fictional characters".

"Let it be," she would hit back. Reading is not only her hobby but a part of who she is.

When we came to the close of the academic year, after playing hide and seek with the school rules, she wrote me a letter, placed it in an old envelope, dropped it in her favorite book, and gave it to me as a GIFT.

"Please, promise me that you going to read it when you get home" she said as she handed it to me in front of the church, after our usual morning devotion on Friday.

I was tempted to tear the envelope open when I got to my dormitory room, but I only read the book and placed the letter in the corner of my handbag, which I will take home to Purosa. On Thursday of the following week, we closed for the year. We travelled on the same bus to town, where she got on a bus along with those students who would be going to Lae. She secured a window seat, left her bag with a friend, and came out, hugging me for the second and third time, saying, "Please, Avundigi, take care", and headed back in as the bus was already full.

Her eyes were filled with emotional tears, and she couldn't wave from the window even though it had been left opened wide. I stood and watched as the bus left the bus stop and accelerated out of sight. At around 11 a.m. I strolled down to West Goroka, where I got on a truck calling for passengers to Okapa. I arrived home late that day. The road was terrible, and I had to walk from Okapa Station down to Purosa in the dark. When I reached home, it was 10pm. I was exhausted when I sat down beside the fireplace, like a piece of wood offshore.

Three days later, I was reminded of my shortcomings; the letter from Michaellyn in my school bag. When I enquired, the bag was on the line, after being washed by my mother. I was very disappointed, thinking that the letter was soaked in water. Fortunately, my mother, filled with wisdom, checked before she did the laundry, and saved it, but she never opened it, and I was saved from the harsh punishment that would follow. She gave it to me and asked what it was. I said it was a letter from the school administration to be given to our parents. I'll read it to you, and I dictate the wrong thing to her, pretending that it was a school fee notice that it was paid in full.

I carried the letter, ran onto a large rock sleeping next to our house where we go for recreation, and opened the envelope. It was all decorated with red hearts and roses, with neat handwriting. Attached to the corner was her photo, from two years ago, at Lae War Cemetery.

As I read through to the very last page, my heart was partly broken, not for Michaellyn, but for myself. We were unconsciously saving each other. I saved her from the paralysis of self-isolation and loneliness. And she unconsciously saved me from running away from myself, from the thought of committing suicide, for how I lived seemed so terrible. I lived a horrible life, like someone was putting a sword on my neck that would be chopped off if I made a tiny error and crossed the line.

This is what she wrote:

Dear Avundigi

This letter with my ugly handwriting may not be pleasing and may taste bitter-sweet as you try to understand. Yet it has the power to give life to a long distance between us for the rest of our lives if you decide to close your heart. And so, I asked that you read with an open heart.

Though we seem to have a lot in common and have come this far, I am far away from you. Not only in the way we look at certain things, but how I was raised as a teenager has a greater impact on my life, and as I get closer to you, I'm afraid I might hurt you as well as ruining our relationship.

For the past few months, since I came to know you, I tried to tell you, but I was afraid, not for your rejection, but I was afraid of losing myself.

Avundigi, I don't love myself. Tell me, how can I love you?

And if I do, will you love me back?

If I can tell the story of my life, the scars that have shaped me, the battle I've fought and won.

Will you love the bruises behind my smile, the pain behind my eyes?

Will you, like the sound of running water, listen to the midnight screams of my life?

Avundigi, I'm sorry for the way I love you, please forgive me.

And let me know if you love me back.

Michaellyn Denevi — Kabiufa High School

I folded the letter, placed it nicely into my back pocket, and like a snail, slowly went back to our cold house, threw the envelope away, and placed the letter between the pages of the reading book she gave to me. Then I went to the kitchen.

My mother was peeling the sweet potatoes and threw them into the boiling water over an open fire. I never said anything, for my heart was troubled by what I had read. I sat quietly beside the fireplace and asked that they bring me the pineapple from the Faith Garden nearby, which my younger sister,

Hanilo, did immediately. We ate, and for the rest of the evening, we told other stories with so much fun, and I was healed from the fear that resulted from reading the letter. My two grandmothers, from a neighboring village, also came, and the day ended with heartwarming tok-ples songs from the Pamusa Community.

Lae, Morobe Province, is not on the other side of Jordan, so we could not just dive to swim across and see each other. I was lost in the thick jungle of Okapa. Close in my heart, it was unknown to me that down in the valley of Markham, someone was skipping meals, hardly going to bed at night, dreaming that I should knock at her door, asking for roasted peanuts, my favorite, or a creamed taro, for that matter. And it never happened, it was just a dream, an illusion, she had to wake up immediately.

February 28, 2005.

The moon was still sleeping when I woke up. My father was in the kitchen reading his lesson to take the morning devotion while waiting for my mother, who was preparing my breakfast to be eaten along the way. I had to leave the village before dawn to catch the truck along the way, so I got up early. Around the fireplace were my loving mother and father, whom I loved to call Papa and Mama. It was an emotional scene to see my mother always in tears when I tried to leave the house for studies somewhere far away.

Between her tears, she would say, "Son, be safe on the way, in a faraway place, we couldn't stop you when you craved for a better education beyond the mountains," and cry. My small brother and sister were still in deep sleep when I left home. Accompanied by my father, we headed into the dark, hoping to reach the lookout mountain called Ivati, before daybreak, where my father would leave me and return home.

I shared my story here because there is no difference when it comes to Michaellyn. The experience is just the same, how sad it has been. We were reunited at the school for another academic year. I was to do grade 11 and she was to do grade 10. We were focused on our studies, so the relationship was not treated as something special that we should spend much time on.

Chapter 6

Memories at Lae War Cemetery

June 2005

One afternoon after dinner in the dining hall, Michaellyn tried to pick up a dish from the table when a few photos of her accidentally slipped from her reading book and fell onto the wooden floor. They were childhood photos taken at the Lae War Cemetery. I picked them up and looked at them. I saw that the place was breathtakingly beautiful and worth visiting. Though I had been to Lae before, as a child with my father, I had never been to the War Cemetery.

She became very excited when I suggested that maybe, before we left this place, we could visit the Lae War Memorial site. That was in June. We made plans, set the dates, and agreed that it would be after her 10th-grade examinations since we didn't have enough time during the term breaks.

"We should focus on our studies first, like putting pebbles in a jug," she suggested.

We supported each other academically until the very end, and in October, she finally sat for her national examination. When she walked out of the examination hall, she came and met me at the bus stop near the large rain tree. The first word she said was, "Avundigi, please, don't forget," and smiled.

"I know," I replied with a faint smile as we walked toward the market to buy something to eat. That day, she wore her most beautiful smile when she was with me, even though her heart felt heavy. I urged her to go and get ready, as they would be leaving the dormitory that day. She waved at me as she crossed the Highlands Highway, hurrying to pack her bag and head to the bus stop.

Many girls were coming in and out of the dormitory, and I felt quite embarrassed standing there, so I walked back to the boys' dormitory. When I returned, she was already waiting for me at the bus stop. The bus to town could arrive at any moment, and we were in a rush. I told her plainly that if I didn't make it to Lae, I would be going home, and we would have to find another time, maybe next year, for the Lae War Memorial trip. She agreed and said her final goodbyes, wishing me the best for the few weeks I would remain on campus.

I stayed at school until the very last day before the holiday. I found myself caught at a crossroads: should I go to Lae or head home? I sent a message to my uncle, who was working with SVS in Lae, and he agreed that I should come down and spend Christmas with him. I knew Michaellyn would be waiting for me. But I had no idea how I was going to find her in such a big city. At the same time, I kept thinking about going home and helping my parents to harvest coffee beans as it was in season. I sat under a tree, gathered my thoughts, and let my heart decide what my mind was struggling to put the piece together.

I knew someone, Delphine from Morobe, who's my classmate, who also knew Michaellyn. I needed her help. She was kind and easy to get along with, so I made up my mind to ask for her help. The next day, I met her after class and told her about my plan to find Michaellyn in Lae.

"I know exactly where she lives!" she said excitedly and offered to help me.

"I'm lucky to have met you," I told her as she carried her books back to the dormitory.

When we officially closed the 2005 academic year, I got on a bus heading to Lae with Delphine. The day was dull, with mist crawling on the highway. The driver took extra caution as the roads were slippery. We arrived late in the evening, just as the rain began to pour, as if someone had left a pressurized tap open and running.

Delphine and I planned that she would find Michaellyn the next day, let her know I was in Lae, and the following day, we would meet in front of Papindo at Eriku. As Delphine went home, I went straight to Kamkumung, then to Awagasi, where my uncle lived.

The following day, I was the first to arrive at the Papindo Supermarket in Eriku. I walked to the overhead bridge and back, went in and out of the shop, but there was no sign of them. I waited for another hour until Delphine finally arrived, alone. As soon as I saw her, I rushed over to meet her.

"Michaellyn is on her way from Markham. Her uncle told me. At first, I got discouraged and went home, but then I decided to come here just in case you're here... and here you are, still waiting," Delphine reported.

"Then, how about on Tuesday?" I suggested.

I couldn't wait to see Michaellyn. We both agreed to meet at the same spot at the same time on Tuesday, and then went our separate ways. On Tuesday, I hopped on a bus to Eriku, filled with doubts and unspoken wishes. I didn't rush as I normally would. Instead, I kept my heart at peace as I crossed the road. When I arrived, only Delphine was there. Before she could tell me where Michaellyn was, the shop doors opened, and Michaellyn walked out, holding two ice cream cones. When she saw me standing there, she froze for a second.

"Namako!" she screamed at the top of her voice and threw the cones of ice cream away, and they landed in the drain!

"Mickey," I mumbled. Mindlessly, she ran toward me. We exchanged warm hugs and firm handshakes, saying nothing. Some things were better left unsaid. Then, without hesitation, we went back inside the shop and each of us got our favourite ice cream flavours before heading toward the field.

There, I thanked Delphine, who was already becoming a close friend.

"You're clever for using Delphine to find me," Michaellyn said. "I don't think we would have found each other otherwise."

"There was no one else I could trust," I replied, looking at Delphine, who was already smiling at me against the wind.

After her exams, Michaellyn had gone to Markham to wait for the school to close so she could come to Lae and wait for me. We only had a few days left before I had to return to Goroka. She thoughtfully proposed a plan to meet again the day after tomorrow.

On Wednesday, she came with Delphine. The best team of three. We took a bus into town, where we said goodbye to Delphine, who had other plans that day. Now, it was just the two of us.

Without wasting time, we headed straight to the Lae War Cemetery. A place of dreams. When we arrived, there weren't many people around, and Michaellyn thought it was perfect. As we walked up to the monument that housed the names of all the fallen soldiers and the countries they fought for, she led me to the right side, where the Australian soldiers were buried. I kid you not, the place was breathtaking. I could barely lift my feet. We walked from grave to grave, and found beautiful names, the date they fell, it was a great moment. We sat at the foot of the white monument, which had a hexagonal base and stood several meters tall. It was there that she told me, in detail, what you read in Part One.

I didn't say a word. My heart shattered hearing it firsthand, from her own lips. My throat tightened, and I lowered my head in respect. She spoke confidently, as if it had all happened on a carpeted floor. But I knew this was how they hid their pain, behind their irresistible smiles and unmatched confidence.

"Namako, this is your favourite place. Thank God no one else is here. I know when we leave, you'll remember us—me and you, only us."

"I'm terrible at keeping memories, but this one, I'll keep," I promised her. We stood and walked toward the other side of the graveyard, heading for the gate and left the site.

During the weekend, she took me to places she thought I might find interesting. We strolled through the streets of the University of Technology in the early morning, ending our day by the beach near Voco Point. My days slipped away like fine sand on the shores of Morobe, passing gently through my fingers until I had only a few left before my trip back to Goroka.

The day before I left, I told her I would be leaving the next day. She was saddened that my time in Lae had passed so quickly, but I had plans to go home before returning to school for another academic year. I only revealed the exact time of my departure in case she wanted to say goodbye.

I spent my last few days with my uncle's family, not seeing Michaellyn until the day of my departure.

That morning, I was already on the bus at Eriku when she came searching for me among the buses calling for passengers to Goroka. When she finally found me, she greeted me with a quiet "Good morning," and begged me to stay for one more day, but it wasn't possible. She stood close to the window until the bus finally left the bus stop. Through the open window, she grabbed my favourite jacket and walked away with it.

After refuelling, we hit the Highlands Highway at midday. My mind was preoccupied with the memories we had made in Lae. I knew she must have felt the same way. I spoke to no one on the bus and didn't buy anything for lunch when we stopped at Umi Market. I only had two cans of pineapple-flavoured Fanta and a few packets of Chicken Snax Michaellyn had bought for me in Lae, knowing they were my favourite. I didn't want to eat them yet. I wanted to take them home and have them on my way to Okapa.

That day, Michaellyn retraced our footsteps at the Lae War Cemetery. She avoided the gravesites we had visited, instead staring at them from a distance, hoping that, in some way, I was still there. The guards thought she was drunk and approached her, but she wasn't, just lost in thought. She spent the final hours of the day sitting under the trees with her book, not reading, only travelling in her mind, following me in her thoughts. She gazed at the sky, watching the eagle and the sparrow play hide-and-seek in the shadows of the clouds before finally heading home. Her heart was heavy, and the only way she could escape the chaos in her mind was by reading. I had heard her say more than once that reading had saved her more than anything else ever could when life hit her hard.

Chapter 7

Love on the Mountain Top

Sunday, 19 February 2006.

Michaellyn returned to Kabiufa Adventist High School from Lae for another academic year. She had already gone through the exhausting registration process on Monday and still had some outstanding fees to pay. Akaliah couldn't afford everything she needed. The little money her uncle, David, had given them was already spent on bus fare and other necessities, covering only 75% of the required fees.

As evening approached and everyone left, a chilly breeze rushed through the campus, and it became cold, as it always did. Silence then filled their hearts as their minds drifted back home. Hunger killed Akaliah, but she didn't tell Michaellyn about it. Their quiet thoughts were interrupted by a mother and her granddaughters from Kabiufa village, who approached them and asked where they would spend the night since it was getting dark.

Akaliah tried to answer, but her throat was blocked. Michaellyn explained that she had already registered to stay in the dormitory and suggested that they take her mother in for the night since she would be travelling back to Lae the next day. That grandma's kindness was a great relief.

The mother and her two young grand-daughters took Akaliah to their home, which was close to the school. As Michaellyn watched her mother walk away with strangers, she hesitated. Then, she turned at the gate and ran back to catch up with them. She met them at the House Line Bus Stop and told them that she had changed her mind; she wanted to spend one last night with her mother. The next day, Akaliah journeyed back to Lae.

A week passed, and Michaellyn started looking for me. There was no one she could ask. I was still in the village. Why would someone return to school after a long Christmas holiday and immediately ask for a boy? It would be embarrassing. No one would do that. She sat alone in a crowd, feeling lonely. There was no sign of me. Disheartened, she returned to the dormitory, cold-hearted.

I returned from the village on Wednesday, but I spent the night in town and arrived on campus on Thursday to register for my final high school year, as the registration was still going on. For the next few days, I kept to myself, not hiding from anyone, not even Michaellyn, but from my thoughts. I locked myself in the dormitory, avoiding the world outside. We didn't see each other that entire week. My heart longed for her, but I decided to follow my mind instead.

On Saturday, after the church service, she spotted me leaving the building through the left-hand door toward the boys' dormitory. She called out fearfully from the lamb shelter, but some of her words were lost in the wind. I heard someone calling my name, though, and I stopped near the bell as she approached me.

The first thing she said was, "Avu! I've been looking for you. Why are you hiding from me? You're running away from me." She gave me a firm handshake, a gold handshake, so tightly that I could feel the longing in her touch. Her voice told me everything. She didn't just miss me the way a girl misses someone she loves; she missed someone who believed in her, someone who encouraged her to keep going, no matter how difficult the journey seemed.

After chatting for a while, I assured her, "We'll be here for the whole year. You can go back to the dormitory."

She turned and walked away, and I headed straight to the boys' dormitory.

The following week the classes began, and we focused entirely on our studies. We didn't abandon our relationship, but we made a rule: 'Education First'

Our education had to come first. Nothing could interfere. Putting pebbles in the jug first should be our sole priority.

During this time, I came to know Michaellyn better. An ambitious and kind-hearted girl, she was adventurous and loved to travel, though she preferred doing so alone or with a close friend. She rarely spoke while travelling, only smiling. I never fully understood this silence, but I suspected it stemmed from what she had been through as a child. Even after being in a relationship with her for some time, I still struggled to understand her quiet nature. I tried every day to figure out why she cut conversations short. Eventually, I realized that her silence spoke volumes. She was not an ordinary girl.

I never understood why she loved the colour green instead of red or purple. But one thing she was passionate about and wanted me to love as well was hiking. She loved being adventurous, visiting new places, talking to different people, learning about their cultures, and understanding their way of life.

On Sundays, when other students left for long weekends, we would hike the mountains of Kabiufa, the ones closest to the school. One day, a local friend of mine took us to the mountain's peak. We followed narrow trails, crawled through rabbit holes, and finally emerged at the summit, where we had a breathtaking view of the school, Daulo Pass, and an aerial glimpse of Goroka Town. It was refreshing, and to this day I still hold on to those memories close to my heart.

In one of our Geography classes, Mr Nicoles shared his experience on climbing Mt. Wilhelm, the highest mountain in the country. He had slipped and fallen, saved only by a pile of rocks that injured his kneecap. The injury was so severe that he couldn't continue the climb and was left unable to walk long distances or run. He also had to confess to the whole class that the injury has ended his rugby career as well.

Over the weekend, Michaellyn and I met behind the administration building, which faced the national highway. And as we watched vehicles and trucks pass by, she told me about her week at the workline. When I turned around, I spotted Mr Nicoles limping toward the school canteen. I told Michaellyn about Mr Nicoles failed journey up at Mt. Wilhelm and the injury that had resulted from it. She was intrigued. We changed the subject, and I shared what I knew and had read about Mt. Wilhelm. She became even more interested.

Then she said, "Since this is your final year, maybe during the third-term break, we should hike Mt. Wilhelm."

I smiled to myself, thinking she was kidding, but she was completely serious. I disagreed, but she kept persisting and we made a plan. We shouldn't go alone. We should invite other students who were interested in joining us. I told some of my friends, and while many wanted to come, most of them, being final-year students, couldn't make it. Two boys, however, were eager to join us; one of them was my cousin, Lindon, from Chuave in Chimbu. He had been to

Mt. Wilhelm before; he knew the area well and had family there, which would be helpful.

Michaellyn said five girls wanted to come, but she noted, "Two of them are very fat, and I don't think they'll be able to climb."

"Then you must stop them," I told her, and she did, and they changed their minds and stayed back. Then we're left with three girls, Hannah, Delphine, and Gracelyn. Delphine and Gracelyn were from Morobe, while Hannah was from the Eastern Highlands. Hannah was an old friend of Michaellyn's from Bena Top Up Primary School, and they had reunited at Kabiufa, becoming best friends again. Hannah and I were from the same village, and she was like a sister to me. She knew about the bond between Michaellyn and me. She was the one who told me a lot about Michaellyn.

Gratefully, Mr. Ray, my accounting teacher, heard about the trip and decided to join us. When Michaellyn told the group that we would hike during the third-term break, they were all excited. Before the second-term break, they were reminded to bring everything they would need for the hike. When they returned, they were fully prepared. The school closed for the third-term break on Thursday, allowing students from other provinces to travel by Friday and over the weekend.

Michaellyn and Delphine took the first bus and waited for us in town. Gracelyn, Lindon, Hannah, and I took the second bus and caught up with them there. We decided to spend the weekend at Chuave, where Lindon would pick up his hiking gear before continuing the journey.

Mr Ray would meet us at Kundiawa Town on Sunday, as he had prior commitments on that day. When we boarded the bus, everyone was very excited.

I warned Lindon, "Don't stay quiet. Keep telling us how far we've come and how much farther we have to go."

None of us had ever been there before.

"It's not far," he said as we reached Daulo Top. The bus zigzagged down the winding road, the driver moving cautiously to avoid accidents. By afternoon, we finally reached Chuave District Station. Pointing up to the top of a tall mountain called Nubuni Kingstar, Lindon assured us that we were almost home.

The bus dropped us at Kongo Coffee Junction, and we walked up the hill to Lindon's place. Michaellyn was still energetic and joked with her three friends, Hannah and Gracelyn, saying that we hadn't even reached the foot of Mt. Wilhelm yet, so they had no reason to be tired. They didn't say a word.

Hannah started eating the Snax biscuits she had bought in town. I was lucky enough to snatch one piece from the packet before she chased me away, telling me to eat from my bag.

"Good sisters never chase their brothers away," I mumbled as I bit into the biscuit. It was indeed crunchy and irresistible.

When we reached the village, Lindon told us to be quiet, and we obeyed, walking silently past every household until we arrived at his home, next to the church. His mother greeted us warmly; his father was in the church. She was welcoming and kind, smiling beautifully and hugging each of us. She quickly peeled some bananas and boiled them over an open fire in their kitchen. During dinner, Michaellyn asked if we could trade. She wanted to swap her banana for my taro, saying she hadn't had taro, her favourite, since they left Finschhafen many years ago, so I gave my taro to her.

I had already told Lindon not to mention Michaellyn to my aunt, but he didn't listen. While we were still eating, he leaned over and whispered to his mother about her. She turned, looked at Michaellyn, and hugged her for a long time. Then, she told her not to worry, she was welcome in our home. Michaellyn, always friendly, already felt accepted into my family. Once we had settled in, Lindon reminded his parents about what he had told them during the holidays. They allowed him to join us but warned us to be careful since we were students.

Lindon's father, who had been to Mt. Wilhelm before, shared a little about the mountain. He told us what to expect and described his own experience. He assured us that our adventure would be unforgettable, though he avoided mentioning too many dangers, he didn't want to scare us. We spent the weekend there, and on Sunday morning, Lindon got ready, and we walked down to the main road.

My aunt was very concerned about us and reminded Lindon to take good care of Michaellyn and the girls. While we waited for a truck, she reassured Michaellyn, telling her to look after herself and to visit her whenever she wanted. She even suggested that Michaellyn spend long weekends or holidays with them since it was much closer than travelling to Lae. She didn't know what she was saying.

We caught a coaster bus from Chuave and arrived in Kundiawa at 10 AM, earlier than I had expected. There were many routes up to Mt. Wilhelm, but we chose to travel via Keglsugl so we could enjoy the beautiful countryside along the way. We spent an hour in Kundiawa waiting for Mr. Rex, who was on his way from Goroka. When he arrived, he apologized for the delay, explaining that the bus he was on had mechanical issues, and they had to stop several times to fix it.

While waiting for our transport, Gracelyn suddenly fell ill, developing a high fever and an upset stomach. She admitted that she had been feeling unwell since morning in Chuave but hadn't said anything. Lindon suggested she return home and wait for us in Chuave. She agreed and left, but when we returned, Lindon's parents told us she had never arrived. We later learned that she had travelled to Goroka and then to Lae, which left everyone of us feeling distressed.

After Gracelyn left, we continued waiting until an old white Land Cruiser from Keglsugl finally arrived. Looking at the condition of the vehicle, I was filled with doubt, but Lindon was confident. We got on along with other passengers, though the truck was also carrying heavy loads of cement bags, making our journey slow, though at least faster than a snail. We left Kundiawa Town at 2pm. The countryside road to Keglsugl was breathtaking as we ascended higher and higher. We drove past incredible caves hidden in the rocky cliffs, crystal-clear waters flowing under wooden bridges, and dark green hills with steep mountains. When we reached Keglsugl, we found a cozy guesthouse near the old airstrip.

Lindon had arranged for us to stay with his friend Jacob, whom we were asked to call Brother Angra. He lived next to a church and welcomed us warmly. He offered us fresh passion fruit and tea before bed. Knowing we had a big day ahead; we went to sleep early.

Before sunrise the next morning, I woke Michaellyn up, and we took a quiet walk around the airstrip, letting the morning dew soak our feet. We could feel the excitement building up in our veins. Mt Wilhelm is the tallest peak in the country, with its majestic view from its highest peak. We killed that day by sightseeing around the surrounding places and hills. We got our feet dirty with Wilhelm's mud, and our mind was focused on another day.

With a lot of excitement already filling the air, Jacob led the way, followed by Michaellyn and

Delphine, after me, Lindon, and Mr. Rex, we set out on a long-awaited and wonderful adventure to conquer Mt Wilhelm. Michaellyn was determined and adventurous, she only wished we had a camera where we could take pictures of such beautiful places. Jacob was an experienced person who led us with a determined spirit. He knew how to keep us from losing sight of distance, but to enjoy every step that we took as we went higher. He was funny and full of stories, and he told us about what to expect and what had happened to some of the travelers in the past. He knew them all very well, he was a skilled guide, an experienced mountaineer who led the way with so much confidence in himself and us as well.

We walked through treacherous paths and cliffs and arrived at the first lake called Piunde. It took us approximately two hours. We were already tempted to rest, but Jacob suggested that we rest at the second lake, which was just a short climb from the first lake. We continued and arrived at the second lake, where we sat down on the piles of rocks and wooden benches, had a light lunch, drank some water, and ate some passion fruits. Michaellyn would pinch my arm and shoulders to see some of the waterfalls and other breathtaking sights she found interesting.

When we sat down, we felt that we were getting cold. I couldn't even dip my hands into the lake as it was as cold as ice. As we were sitting there, I walked around the lake and the surrounding hills, I was lost in the beauty of the lake. I climbed up the low hill and signaled Michaellyn. She came and I showed her some heart-melting sights, where the clouds rested on top of the distant mountains, and showed her the American war plane that had crashed. We were told that the plane crashed in 1944 during World War II. She was very pleased, and I could tell she loved the trip she had planned. We decided to continue the climb on the next day, so we returned to the camp.

In the middle of the night, around 1 a.m. Jacob woke every one of us up, Michaellyn was already awake before Jacob. We had breakfast while it was still dark, and some were waiting outside for others who were still getting themselves ready. Michaellyn moved closer to me and took my hand, she held it firmly and whispered' "Namako, I pray that maybe someday, we could come back for another adventure, just us, you and I, by ourselves. After we complete our studies".

"We'll come back, hopefully," I assured her.

When everyone came out, we were up for another day's hike. A hike that would lead us to the summit. The weather was pleasant, but the problem we faced was the leader. We didn't have enough leaders, for we were travelling at 1 a.m. while it was still dark. Someone has to go ahead and then provide a light for others at the back. In this way, we passed some of the sights. We wished it was during the day so we could see them more clearly.

As we continued to climb, the sky was getting clearer and brighter. The raw wind blew. The day was about to break on the mountain peak. We knew we were taking a greater risk to hike on that mountain, but we also knew that good things and the best view come only to those who take greater risks in life. The path was narrow with steep rocks. If you made one silly mistake, your name would be erased forever from the book of the living. We all were warned of unexpected goodbyes.

We finally arrived at the summit and took a deep breath; the sun was still behind the horizon. Michaellyn, who was sitting close to me, read out loudly, "4509 m".

Slowly, the sun made its way through the horizon and painted the sea of clouds that were sleeping on top of the mountains with yellow and red, making it one of the best and memorable sights. I turned around, it wasn't an accident, Michaellyn turned towards me swiftly, we stared at each other for a while, and she kisses the skies with the kisses of her sweet lips for the first time. She kissed the one she loved on the highest peak, and she made a promise when there were no clouds to hide the face of the sun, when it poured its rays full strength on us:

"No matter how far this relationship will go,

how long it will last, Namako,

I'm not losing you, not even for a minute.

I'm keeping it close,

very close to my heart."

It had been a wonderful and unforgettable experience with the girl I'll never stop loving. We could vividly see the two lakes, Aunde and Piunde, popularly known as Male and Female Lakes. Their distant view appeared like a swimming pool painted blue on the surface. Mr. Rex was very excited as it was his first-ever experience as well. He made a promise that when we get back to school, he will host a large party for the Mt. Wilhelm team.

Delphine couldn't keep the raw excitement to herself, but spread out her arms wide and waved to the birds and skies. After I noticed unusual smiles and cute laughter exchanged between the two, Delphine and Lindon, I jokingly said to Lindon, who was already staring at Delphine, "Bro, you going to catch her, or she's going to fly off the cliff and you're going to miss her selfishly for the rest of your life".

He just gave off a blank stare by lifting his eyebrows out of a little guilt and shame, I presumed, but I was wrong.

They have their own stories to tell, I'll save my ink. Looking back, I thought it was just yesterday.

Chapter 8

Class of 2007

"This year will be different; it will never be the same," she whispered to herself. Just a random evening thought between her heart and mind before she climbed into bed and drifted off to sleep. The lights were turned off, and there was total silence in the dormitory, except for the giggles of other girls who were still awake in the darkness. Many had already gone to sleep.

On the first day of school, everyone seemed like strangers. She was a continuing student, so why did she feel like she didn't belong? A simple "Hello" was enough before they passed by. There was a deep longing in her heart, an irresistible desire to see me someday—someday soon, to fill the emptiness and void in her soul.

Michaellyn was a senior student, yet she was selective about her friends. The few good friends she has were enough for the whole year. She prioritized her studies and never allowed distractions. During her final year, she was assigned to work as an office janitor in the English Department. It was in that office, after finishing her tasks, that she read and wrote letters and poems to the one she loved the most. She had a calm personality, hid behind her prettiest smile, and was well-liked by her teachers and other students.

If there was one special soul, more than a sister, a friend, and a schoolmate, that Michaellyn found comfort and healing from, it was Hannah. Hannah and Michaellyn were like one person living in two different bodies. Hannah played her role mindfully and saved their friendship on several occasions. If Hannah were on the basketball court, Michaellyn would be on the sidelines cheering. Wherever Michaellyn was, Hannah would be close by.

Hannah was the first to arrive on campus, got herself registered, and then returned home for reasons only she and her parents knew. She came back a week later. Michaellyn had been wondering about Hannah's absence when she saw her walking up the stairs toward the administration building with her father. Her eyes didn't deceive her; it was Hannah, carrying a black handbag. She wanted to call out her name, but held back. Instead, she walked as fast as she could from the junior block toward the senior block. While Hannah's father was chatting with the deputy principal, Michaellyn ran to her friend, and they greeted each other with a long, warm hug. Their greeting startled the birds nearby and even made the typist peek out of the printing room to see what had happened.

"Hannah, how is he? Please tell me the truth about him. And why are you so late? We started classes a week ago. I've been hoping and waiting for you since the day I arrived on campus."

Michaellyn poured out her worries, her words rushing like a river. But Hannah didn't respond. Instead, she pulled a letter from the bilum she was carrying and handed it to her.

Michaellyn lost her breath when she saw the sender's name on the envelope, which was an old one, probably taken from an old box. She tore it open in front of Hannah and read it silently, her heart melted with a wide smile. Hannah, meanwhile, was plucking tiny weeds from the gravel when she suddenly received unexpected playful punches from her friend as she read the letter.

The letter read:

Dear Michaellyn,

Greetings from the heart of Purosa.

I hope you're well and already settled in school for your final year of high school.

I am doing great here, but I want you to know that I'll be staying in the village this year.

Hannah knows why. If you ask, she will tell you.

I hope to come to town around August.

I know it may seem far away, like an eternity, but you'll always be in my heart, closer than you think. But if we don't meet this year, or even for several years, I wish you all the best.

I write this letter to remind you not to let anything distract you from your studies. This is your final year, so, give it your best in everything you do.

Whenever I miss you, I allow my soul to drift back to our old memories while reading the book you gave me.

Your face is engraved in my mind, and I know my heart will never stop longing for you.

Take care until August, if I get the chance to see you again.

Love, Namako

Avundigi Kasah – Okapa District

She read it a second, then a third time. Then she turned to Hannah, expecting her to explain what it meant when he said she would know the reason.

"We have the whole year to talk about that," Hannah said. "Let's go for dinner."

Michaellyn sighed, reading the letter again as she walked, trying to answer the question herself, but she couldn't. Disappointed, she followed Hannah to the dining hall.

In the middle of the night, she was awakened by a strange dream. Once again, she was on the beach in Finschhafen with her father, running against the waves and playing—until a storm came, and engulfed then. The waves erupted like a volcano, and her father vanished like smoke into the raging sea. She sat up in bed, the memories of her father flashing across her mind, and she wept silently.

That night, she made a promise to herself to sacrifice everything for her studies. During the first term, she stayed focused and saw great progress in her academics. Her teachers admired her discipline. She worked diligently in her assigned duties and remained committed to her studies. She built strong mental walls around herself, shutting out distractions. She became unstoppable and filled with love and kindness for others.

She was tempted to go home, to Okapa with Hannah during the first term break, but resisted, choosing instead to stay back and send a letter. When Hannah returned home, she delivered Michaellyn's letter to me. I received it on our way home from church. I was tempted to read it right there while walking, but there were too many people around, so I placed it in my bilum and took a short path home.

I ran onto the large rock near the house and started tearing open the envelope when my mom called me for lunch. Ignoring her, I began reading slowly, sentence by sentence, word by word:

Dear Avundigi Kasah

Greetings from the heart of the country~ Kabiufa.

I received your letter earlier this year, and I was very excited.

I'm well and doing great.

My heart turned cold as ice when Hannah told me why you won't be going to school this year, but take heart, everything happens in its own time. That's what we both believe in.

I was tempted to visit you during the holidays, but I couldn't. I've been waiting for August, and it has felt so long, just as you mentioned, but I'm here, waiting patiently for that day.

I hope to see you soon.

But please, for now, write back and tell me how life in the village is treating you.

Love, Namako

Michaellyn Denevi – Kabiufa High School, 2007

"What are you doing back there, sitting on that bare rock in the heat of the day when I called you for lunch?" my mom yelled at me, while handing me my plate.

"He must be in love with a girl. I saw someone give him a letter on the road," my dad commented from the table just outside the door.

"What's wrong with you guys? So embarrassing," I muttered as I made my way out of the house with my lunch and sat down on the lawn. I loved my dad. He had a way of joking, even when things felt real. He often saved me from my mom's harsh scoldings with his humour.

At the end of the week, I quickly drafted a letter to send to Michaellyn. She'd be waiting. But there was no ink, so I used a pencil, and the middle page of my sister's exercise book. I even tried to draw a heart on the side, but the pencil tore the paper and ruined everything. Frustrated, I rewrote it on a new sheet and sealed it with sticky tape since I didn't have an envelope that night. I thought about searching my father's box for one, but it was the middle of the night, and I was afraid. Foolish of me. The next morning, when I woke up, Hannah had already left. The letter was never sent.

In August, I followed my father into town. We were there to buy stationery for Watai Elementary School back in the village. We arrived on Monday, spent the next two days shopping at different stores in town, and planned to return home on Friday. Since we finished early on Thursday, I asked my father if I could go to Kabiufa to see a friend. He refused, saying he had other plans. I hadn't told him that the friend was Michaellyn. I had already met Lindon in town, so technically, there was no reason for me to go to Kabiufa. Still, August was the only month in the year I insisted on seeing Michaellyn. Yet, I didn't want to disobey my father. I was caught in between.

At around 3 pm, he changed his mind and allowed me to go up to Kabiufa. We stood at the bus stop, waiting for the bus to arrive so he could see me jump on a bus, and he would return home. But when the bus finally came, he suddenly changed his mind and decided to come with me. How could I stop him? How could I meet Michaellyn with my father watching? I was at war in my mind the entire journey to the school.

When we arrived, we met Lindon and chatted for a while. Quietly, I asked him if he had seen Michaellyn recently.

"I saw her this morning at breakfast. She might be in the dormitory. Maybe we should check with the other girls," he suggested. What we didn't know was that, at that very moment, she was already in town looking for me, anxiously and helplessly. Lindon had told her two days ago that he saw me in town.

By the time we reached the main gate to find her, a bus had just dropped her off at the house line bus stop, and she walked towards the dormitory. As she got closer, she recognized me and called my name, but the wind carried her voice away. She picked up her pace, walking faster to reach us under the large rain tree near the road at the crossing. When she reached me, she hugged me shamelessly, without fear of who was watching. Her eyes were filled with emotional tears that never wanted to fall but welled up.

Then, as she turned around, she noticed my father. Suddenly, she looked a little embarrassed and guilty. But with courage, she reached out her hand, greeted him, introduced herself, and told him that we were best friends. I admired her bravery. She stood her ground and must have earned his respect in that moment. My father, observing everything, the way she reacted, the emotion in her eyes, must have concluded in his mind that I was in love with her. But on our way home, I turned down his assumptions.

"She's just a friend," I told him. He just nodded, giving me a knowing smile.

"A friend, hmm?"

I knew what he was thinking. We had less than two hours together. If my father hadn't been there, Michaellyn would have poured everything out: how much she missed me, what had happened after I left, how she was doing in school. But she couldn't. Not with my father standing there. She could only answer the few questions I asked, and a few from my father.

While we were still there, the bell rang for dinner, and the girls began crossing the Highlands Highway toward the dining hall. She didn't want to leave, but as those who knew me passed by, saying hello on their way to the mess, she grew uneasy and, without a proper goodbye, she handed me three packets of Snax and a can of Fanta then she left. Then I went back to town with my father.

Michaellyn continued her studies and performed exceptionally well. For the next several months, we neither communicated nor saw each other. But the longing to see each other again grew stronger. She had already made up her mind, if I didn't turn up in the coming months, she would find me, wherever she thought I could be. But I never went to town as she had hoped. I didn't even attend her graduation.

The night before her graduation, she cried to herself. She had asked Lindon more than once to relay a message to me to come to her graduation. But I didn't. Hannah's parents came. But I stayed behind. In fact, I wanted to go. I really did. But it was difficult. So, I stayed in the village, helping my mama and papa. I don't know what happened; she never told me either.

Chapter 9

Daybreak at Okapa Station

"Mickey, it's okay, you don't have to do that. You don't have to risk yourself coming with me. I'll tell him everything about you, so please, go home. You already handed me your letters for him. I'll deliver them, I promise. What made you change your mind and ask to come with me?" Hannah begged Michaellyn, while packing their belongings in the dormitory.

Items like the bucket, mattress, tools, and some clothes had already been given to her mother in Kabiufa Village right after she finished her exams. She only had to repack her camping bag, which she did efficiently in less than twenty minutes. Then they came outside, where all the Grade Twelve girls had gathered at the gate under the large eucalyptus tree with their belongings. Some were waiting for their parents, while others got on the buses and left. There were warm hugs and tearful goodbyes, as many knew that they might never see each other again, even for a lifetime.

Hannah sat beside Michaellyn, who used her bag as a pillow and rested her head on it in the cool shade of a large rain tree. She closed her eyes, but her mind stayed awake, urging her to take the risk she had been planning for weeks, to find me. She hardened her heart against Hannah's pleas to go home and wanted to go to Okapa instead.

Michaellyn knew exactly where she needed to go, which PMV to take, how much the trip would cost, and how long it would take to reach me. She feared that she might never see me again. No matter how dangerous, how crazy, or how rough the journey would be, nothing could stop her, not even Hannah.

She woke up, grabbed her bag, and she didn't have much to carry. She said goodbye to her friends and walked straight to the bus stop with Hannah to catch a ride to town. As they crossed the road, a thought struck her: to find Lindon and ask if he could go with them. Hannah waited at the bus stop while Michaellyn hurried down to the basketball court, where she found Lindon. She told him about her plan to go to Okapa with Hannah.

"You're kidding me, young lady. Are you crazy?" Lindon burst out angrily, urging her not to take such a risk. He assured her that I would come to Lae next year to study and that she could meet me there. But she wouldn't listen. Lindon followed her back to the bus stop, and the three of them got on a bus to town.

At West Goroka, Lindon tried one last time to convince her. He begged her to jump off the truck so he could send her on a bus to Lae. But she turned a deaf ear. Seeing that she was determined to go, Lindon paid her bus fare and informed the crew about her. He then ran into a supermarket and bought her lunch. He waited until the truck left for Okapa before heading back to school.

The truck made a quick stop at Faniufa, where passengers usually bought their lunch. Everyone got off except Michaellyn, who stayed inside the truck. Hannah bought her a Fanta and some plastic-wrapped chips, adding to what she already had. As the truck roared down to Paragon and hit the Highlands Highway, Hannah assured Michaellyn that everything would be fine and apologized for trying to convince her to go to Lae instead.

Michaellyn only ate the chips and carefully placed the Fanta in the side pocket of her bag. She then began asking Hannah questions about the places and mountains they passed. Before they reached Olix Market in the Lufa District, one of the truck's back tyres got punctured by a rough pothole.

The crew urged everyone to get off so they could fix the tyre, as it was already getting late. While they stood by the roadside waiting, Pamella, a fellow Grade Twelve student from Kabiufa recognized Michaellyn and Hannah from across the road. She walked over and greeted them. Though they had been boarding students in different classes, they were surprised and happy to see each other. When the tyre was repaired, they got back on the truck and sat together. Pamella asked Michaellyn many questions about where she was headed. She knew Michaellyn was a Morobean.

"She's with me. I'm taking her home for the Christmas holiday," Hannah quickly interrupted and saved the moment. The three girls started reminiscing about their school days, cherishing every memory. They had just left Kabiufa but had so many stories to share. As the sun began to set over the Western Hills, the truck left Kuru Mountain, zigzagging down the steep slopes. The driver, attempting to cross the same river seven times, let go of the brakes and focused on the road towards Okapa Station. The girls had become best friends on the truck. Pamella then suggested that since it was getting late, they could spend the weekend at her place, as the truck would only take them as far as Awande Junction.

When the truck dropped them off at the junction, they travelled on foot past Miarasa Community to Pamella's village, Yasubi, a beautiful place by the roadside. There, Michaellyn and Hannah would spend the weekend with Pamella. The next day was Sabbath, and both girls were Adventists, except for Pamella's mother, who was Lutheran. Early in the morning, Pamella's mother prepared a breakfast of sweet potatoes, sako leaves, and dry mumu-cooked kaukaus from the previous day.

As they ate, Pamella's father reassured the girls, cleared the doubts in their hearts.

"Today, we will go to church." he told them.

"And tomorrow, we will have a feast to celebrate Pamella's safe return from school. Since you are her Grade Twelve friends, the feast will be for you too. Then on Monday, Pamella and I will take you to Ivingoi and send you off with those from Purosa who will be coming to the Monday market."

Pamella was pleased with her father's kindness. Michaellyn and Hannah agreed, and they spent the weekend at Yasubi.

On Sunday, the girls helped prepare the feast, peeling bananas, taros, sweet potatoes, and yams. Pamella's small brother, Awii, helped in fetching water using long bamboo tubes. Pamella's father sneaked off to Okapa Station to buy a carton of lamb flaps and a live chicken from a neighbour. They made a Mumu, grilling the chicken and cooking it in coconut cream over an open fire. At noon, Pamella's mother returned from church and joined them. Pamella's friends were also invited, bringing food to contribute to the feast. Everyone ate, laughed, and celebrated together. Michaellyn and Hannah were given a dish of food each and were deeply grateful for everything Pamella's family had done for them.

On Monday, they climbed the steep hill up to the main road, where Pamella's mother bade them farewell and returned home. Pamella, her small brother Awii, and her father accompanied Michaellyn and Hannah down to Ivingoi. Along the way, Michaellyn was touched by the warm greetings of strangers passing by. At midday, they arrived at Ivingoi Marketplace. The road was filled with people from the south, selling fresh fruits and vegetables at cheap prices. Michaellyn was impressed and bought heaps of peanuts, and filled her bag, to be eaten along the way.

Pamella kept an eye out for anyone travelling from Purosa, but unfortunately, she couldn't find anyone. They walked past the market and stopped opposite the Ivingoi Provincial High School gate. Hannah reassured Pamella and her father that they could walk the rest of the way alone and that they didn't need to worry. Michaellyn hugged Pamella tightly and promised to see her again. She thanked Pamella's father for everything, and then she and Hannah started walking towards Purosa.

As they climbed Yavavari Hill, the landscape became familiar, and Michaellyn remembered everything I had told her.

"When you reach the mountaintop, after coming through the jungle road, you'll see a village on the plateau. That's home. That's Purosa."

She could now recognize the back of the mountain, and Hannah confirmed it. Michaellyn felt like she was going home, somewhere she truly belonged. They hurried into the jungle road and arrived at the lookout point on top of the mountain called Ivaty.

"I can see him down there!" Michaellyn exclaimed jokingly.

Hannah burst out laughing and sat on the thick,

carpeted lawn to rest. From there, they could clearly see smoke rising from the gardens. Pointing in the direction starting from the church towards the left, Hannah showed Michaellyn where they needed to go. While they were there, a crowd of people, young and old, some carrying babies, others with bags of rice, hurried past them. They looked different and spoke a language that Michaellyn immediately recognized as unfamiliar. She knew it wasn't Pamusa Tokples.

After the group passed, Hannah pointed beyond the overlapping blue mountain ranges to tell Michaellyn, "That is where they are going, they will spend the night in the forest before they reach their village," she explained.

Michaellyn didn't say a word. Her feet ached from the pebbles and gravel, and she was exhausted. She had never walked such long distances before. This was an experience she would never forget. Before they stood up to leave, Hannah turned to Michaellyn and spoke seriously.

"For as long as you intend to stay, you'll have to stay with me. This trip wasn't planned with Avundigi. His parents are there, his family are there, and the community is watching. For the good of everyone, you'll stay at my house. We're neighbours with Avundigi. We'll visit him. We'll go to his house this afternoon. Or, if he hears that I'm home, you might just find him standing at the door."

Michaellyn slowly understood the gravity of what Hannah was saying. She agreed and thanked her. She knew she wouldn't have made it this far without her friend. From that point on, the journey wouldn't be as difficult, it was all downhill. The two girls strolled along the muddy road and soon reached the first village called Takai-Purosa. Michaellyn knew that after passing the fourth village, she would finally reach my place. They greeted the people they met along the way. Everyone was welcoming and kind.

As they walked past a few houses along the roadside, they arrived at a village called Weneru. The atmosphere felt different. Hannah knew this was my uncle's place, but she didn't tell Michaellyn. My grandmother was there, selling sweet potatoes and cabbages. She immediately recognized Hannah as a student from Kabiufa High School. Hannah also knew she was my grandmother when the old woman left everything to come and greet them. The other women sitting behind their garden produce just smiled and waved.

After chatting for a moment, my grandmother ran back, grabbed some cabbages, and handed them to

Michaellyn.

"This is my friend; she's here for the holidays." Hannah introduced Michaellyn. Michaellyn, who couldn't speak Tokples, smiled and greeted my grandmother in Pidgin. But my grandmother, who didn't speak Pidgin, responded in her language. What a tragedy.

Michaellyn just smiled, nodding as if she understood. They continued down the rocky slope toward the river that crossed the road, then climbed the next hill leading up to the rugby field. That was where they received the warmest greetings. They were home. On the field, some boys were playing rugby touch. Unknown to them, I was among the players. As they walked past me, they didn't recognize me, I was just another boy in the field. Michaellyn was exhausted from the long walk. As they approached Watai Elementary School and climbed the low hill to my village, she turned to Hannah and said to her, "Let's not go to his house yet."

Hannah's family had been expecting her that Monday. The moment they arrived, all her younger siblings ran to her, jumping and clinging onto her in excitement. After the welcome greetings, Hannah introduced Michaellyn to her family.

"This is my high school friend from Morobe. She's here to spend Christmas with us," she informed them. Her family was impressed and made Michaellyn feel welcome.

Before dusk, Hannah showed her around the surrounding villages. She even showed her the mountaintop where they had rested earlier. But despite everything, Michaellyn still hadn't seen me. She didn't know how or when it would happen, or what she would say. But there was a raw excitement buried in her heart.

Turning around, Hannah pointed towards a traditional house in the middle of the coffee trees. They could see the smoke rising from the kitchen.

"That's his home. Do you see the smoke?" Hannah teased Michaellyn. "He must be cooking for you."

Michaellyn poked her side and told her not to joke about it.

Meanwhile, I had just finished a game and was thirsty. I ran up to the water tap near Hannah's house, where I met her mother, who was fetching the water.

"Hannah is home, with her Morobean friend," she told me. My heart skipped a beat at the mention of the name Morobe. Hannah had many friends from Morobe, including Michaellyn. But I never imagined it could be her. The thought troubled me so much that instead of going to see them, I turned and ran home. Hannah, Michaellyn, and I would be in serious trouble if anyone in Hannah's or my family found out. Hannah understood this better than I did.

That evening, when Hannah's mother returned home with bottles of water, she casually mentioned that she had met me at the tap. Hannah was troubled and deep in thought, but pretended to be okay. Michaellyn, however, was at war with herself. Her heart skipped a beat as if the earth itself was shaking. She sat quietly, barely listening as Hannah told them about what happened along the way and why they spent the weekend at Yasubi. The treatment they received from Pamela's parents, the party on Sunday.

That night, both of them were tired because of a long walk. Michaellyn was the first to go to bed. The next morning, before sunrise, Hannah's mother woke up and prepared breakfast. Michaellyn also woke up and sat beside an open fire. As they sat around the fireplace, she told Michaellyn about the place, the number of villages, the weather, and the kinds of food they grew.

Pretending to ask innocently, Michaellyn inquired, "How many kids from this place are at Kabiufa?"

She just wanted to hear my name.

The first name Hannah's mother mentioned was someone who lived next door. But then she added,

"He'll be here to see Hannah."

When the sun rose over the mountain, everyone got up and gathered around the fire, trying to keep themselves warm. Michaellyn kept an eye out on the doorway way hoping for a visitor's knock. But it took so long, and no one turned up. She had to be patient. Hannah's parents and some of the children left for the garden. Only Hannah and Michaellyn stayed behind. Hannah saw this as an opportunity and took Michaellyn to my house right in between the coffee trees.

At that moment, I was at the fish pond, digging around the water's edge, when my younger sister ran up to me, breathless and excited at the same time.

"Hannah is here to see you. There's another girl as well," she announced, folding her arms behind her back. She had noticed the other girl with her. I was covered in mud, both my hands, feet, shoulders, and even parts of my face. But the moment I saw Hannah at the gate, my heart raced. It was Hannah, and next to her was my beautiful love story.

I ran down to the stream, washing the mud off my face in a second before rushing back up. Hannah laughed at my reaction. I wasn't sure if Michaellyn found it funny, too. I hugged Hannah, not just for who she was, but for everything she had done. Then I turned to Michaellyn.

As I wrapped my arms around her, I felt her tears falling onto my shoulder.

She had come a long way.

Just for this hug.

Just for me.

Just for this place.

I was in my right mind and in control of my emotions, but I respected Michaellyn for the way she let her feelings out. Hannah, who was teary as well, couldn't say a word. Michaellyn bowed her head low and tried to uproot the crawling grass with her feet, and also wiped the tears from her eyes with the edge of her T-shirt.

I instructed my younger sister to bring out the chairs from the kitchen, and we sat on the lawn. Evalyn ran down to the river and informed my mom that Hannah had come to see me with an unknown girl. My mother ran up to find them alone sitting on the chair. I was with a knife in the sugar cane garden behind the house. When I returned with sugarcane, I found my mother talking with Hannah and Michaellyn.

My mother knew nothing. I offered them sugar cane, and we sat there chatting. I introduced Michaellyn to my mom confidently, saying that she was my high school best friend and had completed her grade 12 and was here with Hannah to spend the holiday. I never knew that this was what Hannah told Michaellyn on their way home.

My mother went to the garden on Sunday, and we had a bag of sako leaves and cabbages in the kitchen, so she begged Hannah to stay here with me as she would hang the clothes on the line and prepare our breakfast. I sat close to Michaellyn and listened to each of them as they had turns to tell me of what happened and why Michaellyn was here. My heart sank and bled. Michaellyn tried to save, but Hannah told everything, fearing my mom, which Michaellyn never knew. The whole scene was very complicated, yet the three of us sat and unpuzzled it.

Later, Hannah told me of what she told Michaellyn, that she would have to be with her for as many weeks as she wanted to stay. I agreed and we went into the kitchen where my mother was cooking. We told other stories and cool jokes while having breakfast of rice and kumu with fish. My father joined us, and I kid you not; he almost, almost ruined the soup. He had already done the smiling, but I was prepared. I saved the situation in a way you'll never imagine possible. He came and was greeted by Hannah, and right after, I told him what he already knew. He recognized Michaellyn and welcomed her to his home. He added on to tell the two girls to come around sometimes. Hannah agreed, and Michaellyn nodded with a fake smile.

Chapter 10

Endless Love - Okuk Highway

The Highlands Okuk Highway has been, and always will be, the best route not only for tourists and other travelling public but also for the lovebirds without wings who are dominating the skies. Okuk Highway is the longest route in the country. The driving distance from Lae to Goroka is about 295 km.

I've been on that country road before, with my father when I was a child, but the experience was unique and awesome. My father would always take me with him when he decided to travel to Lae. But to ride on that country road together is something Michaellyn and I had been dreaming of and hoping for a long time since we were in high school.

When we got on a PMV bus at the Lae/Madang bus stop near Goroka Main Market, she suggested sitting close to the window, three seats behind the driver. By then, more than half of the passengers were already inside, and it didn't take long for the bus to fill up, as many decided to travel to Lae on that very day. In less than an hour, all the seats on the bus were occupied, and the driver started the engine and moved the bus out from the bus stop to the main road, toward the Puma service station to get refuelled. That is where we paid our bus fares and took to the highway.

The driver made a quick stop at Funiufa, the famous spot where trucks and buses stop to buy lunch while travelling on the Highlands Highway. Michaellyn stayed inside as she didn't want to buy anything for herself. I got off the bus and bought her a plastic bag of chips and four cans of Fanta - pineapple-flavoured was my favourite. She quickly gulped down the first one, as it was already getting hot on the bus. That was the last stop we made. We left Goroka at 10 a.m. and arrived in Kainantu at 11:30 a.m., a 90-minute drive.

The crew, a tall and dark-skinned guy from Kainantu who was also the funniest, kept us alive with his rude jokes to Kol Wara, where we got some fish, peanuts, and bananas. We stood further away from the bus, and as she beheld the beauty of the Yonki Dam sleeping down the hill, she turned and looked steadily at me. Our eyes met. She tried to smile but held it back, giggling to herself before she got up and said, "Hey Avundigi, I think I'll be going far away from you next year."

"Where do you plan to go?" I asked innocently because I was caught off guard.

I heard what she said clearly, and I didn't want her to finish before I could reply.

"I'll be going to Sonoma Adventist College," she replied.

"I thought we were going to Unitech," I quickly interrupted.

"No, I choose Sonoma Adventist College."

I never said another word but thought to myself, Sonoma? No, Mickey, why? So many miles away. I don't want to live far away from someone I truly love. I knew she felt the same way, but it was the choice she had made, following her passion and goals in life. She had been planning to be a missionary teacher, and Sonoma was where she wanted to go. They provide holistic education there, she thought. I must respect her decision; I can't be a dictator all my life, telling her what to do with her own life, where she wants to go, and what she wants to do.

She knew I was disappointed and became very

sad about the choice she had made. But she was optimistic as well, not for her to change her mind and withdraw from Sonoma, but because I wasn't going to see her for a very long time. We got back on the bus, and the whole trip from Kol Wara to Markham Valley was filled in complicated and unwavering clouds of deep thoughts, puzzling our minds. If I see her again, it will be after four years, which is too long. She assured me not to worry, as things would get better when we approached Umi Market, but I didn't believe what she said.

The bus made another stop at Umi Market, where we bought some peanuts and bananas. I tried to have roasted peanuts, but my stomach gave up on me. She quickly looked for her mother, but she wasn't there, and she asked her relatives if they had seen her, but they told her that her mother had gone down to Lae a few weeks ago. They also told her that David had been looking for her anxiously.

I just stood there watching Michaellyn enjoy the fruits as well as sago, which I didn't like, so I didn't have a bite when she bought one for me.

"Namako, you know what?"

Her smile quickly faded as she spoke while leaning

against the back window of the bus.

"I didn't know what would happen to me when I got home."

"What do you mean?" I interrupted.

She took a deep breath, paused for a minute, and continued.

"I never told my uncle that right after my examination, I'd be going to Okapa with my friend for a few weeks' break".

"That's so stupid," I told her.

"It doesn't concern you; I'm just letting you know. If - if anything happens, I want you to know that nothing, absolutely nothing, would keep me from loving you."

"What do you mean?" I asked after a moment of deep thinking.

"You'll soon find out," she spoke harshly, and got onto the bus. I followed as the driver ignited the engine.

We didn't converse along the way. She was quiet. After several attempts to make her talk, I also kept quiet as we drove for miles and into the city. She had taken a risk she shouldn't have. She broke my heart gracefully. The bus dropped us at Eriku, as it would be returning to Goroka. It was getting late, and I promised to meet her in the coming days. So, I left for Kamkumung, and Michaellyn took the bus home to Tent City.

Chapter 11

Near Painful Heartbreak

I never felt the pain of being in love with someone until I realized that I was about to lose Michaellyn. If not for a while, it would mean forever. I was afraid. I didn't want to let her go; I kept the promise I made to myself, and I held on to it until she took part of me away. If she hadn't gone to my place, the whole drama would have been different. But sometimes, to love is to take a risk. This is how it happened, in a very awful but disciplined way.

"Where have you been?"

An angry voice shouted from the living room. Before she could say a word, David stood up from the sofa with a power cord and, without a word, landed five painful whips below her shoulders, on her left and right arms. She stood there, searing, trying to withstand the pain, but the blood spilled vigorously out from an open cut. He then grabbed her head and hit it against the wall very hard several times until he realized that her nose had started to bleed. He let her fall to the floor.

Furious, David left the house and went outside. He had never done that before, and he felt guilty for what he had done. He resolved to reconcile with Michaellyn but not immediately. Michaellyn was then taken into the bathroom and treated by Lulume. That was the very first pain she had received from her uncle after so many years of living with them.

When everyone gathered at the table for dinner that evening, David attempted to apologize but failed, and warm tears ran down his cheeks. He loved Michaellyn so much. She sat on the other end, with plasters and bandages. Akaliah sat quietly with a cold heart, staring at David, then at Michaellyn. There was total silence in the room as David began to speak after taking a deep breath and wiping the tears away with a handkerchief.

"You know the reasons why you have plasters and bandages on you, don't you?"

Michaellyn nodded.

"When you didn't come home two days after your 12th-grade examination, I risked it all and started looking for you. I called the school, and they didn't know where you were. I asked some students who had come home, and when there was no sign of you, I went to Markham looking for you, hoping that you might have gotten off there. But you weren't there. I took your mother and went to the school; it was heartbreaking when we didn't find you.

"I was stressed and depressed at the same time. Your mother couldn't sleep at night. She was worried and heartbroken. We filed a complaint with the police in Goroka and Lae, and everyone started looking for you. A week later, we learned that you were with a girl from Okapa, is that true?

"During the final moments after the exam, you went with her. I was burning with anger, wondering why you had to do that to me and your mother without letting us know. Your mother lost her mind and was stressed when she learned you had gone missing in the jungles of Okapa. She complained to me about why I had sent you to a faraway school when there were plenty of primary and secondary schools in the city. You have your answers. I'm sorry I reacted aggressively. It will never happen again, I promise."

Michaellyn was in tears when she heard what happened while she was away. She apologized and promised never to do it again. That night, she broke up with me in her heart and deleted her feelings for me without letting me know. She hated herself even more and became bitterly depressed. She couldn't think straight. She made a lot of crazy decisions out of anger and frustration. She chose herself that day. She chose her family, her mother. And that was the best decision she had made. Love will return in another form if it's truly yours, but family must come first.

She kept her distance from me for the next three weeks. We never met, we never talked, and our love was temporarily suspended. I never knew what happened to her. But I recalled what she told me on our way from Goroka, at Umi Market, and it troubled me. I knew she must have been in trouble with her uncle. I was afraid this might happen, and in every way, I've been very careful when it comes to my relationship with Michaellyn. When the wound finally became a scar, she was reminded of what she told me: to love me even in the chaos and brokenness of life's ups and downs.

Three weeks later, we met accidentally inside Papindo, at Eriku. She tried to tell me what had happened, wanting to tell me something, but she was afraid. Yet, I already read it in her eyes. I saw the scar on her face, one that never really healed on her left chin. We never talked about it, as there were many people inside. She wasn't in her right mind either. I never asked why she had the terrible scar, as she was with her friend, who was older than herself. I did not know that she was Lulume, David's wife.

She walked me to the bus stop and asked if it was okay to meet at the church on Sabbath. I agreed, and on Sabbath, we met at Talair SDA Church. Right after the service, we met outside, just beside the large tree. Happy faces and warm smiles filled the area, but her smile dimmed quickly. She was broken. For in her string bilum was a letter with the saddest lines.

It was unknown to me. We chatted for a while, and I asked what happened to her. She was confident enough to tell me what happened, but I was very worried. Before she left, she took out the letter and handed it to me. When I tried to open it and read it in front of her, she snatched it back from my hand and placed it inside the bilum I was carrying.

She never said anything after that. She acted like she had something important to do or an urgent meeting to attend to, and she cut me off with her silence, showing no interest in talking. I lived next to the church, separated by a fence, and all my friends were intimidating, so she left.

I went home disappointed as well. I was tempted to read the letter right after lunch, but we had visitors, and it was impossible. Later that day, I was asked to scrape the coconut, which I did immediately, and after that, I sat on the coconut scraper and started to read the letter. It was the letter that buried me alive in the darkest grave I dug for myself.

She wrote two pages, thanking me for the time we had together since high school, and now the time had passed for us to part ways. She explained what happened the day she came home. But at the end of the letter, she heartily asked me to wait. She must have meant for me to wait, but when I saw it, it gave me a little glimpse of hope: "I'll wait."

A chance to believe in love again. I sat there, despite a thousand mosquito bites, and the food got cold. I never ate anything when I went to bed, trying to save myself from myself. We had come a long way, and I wasn't ready for this separation. I was hurt, and my heart started to bleed inside. I could feel the pain, the real pain of love and loss.

On the other side, the food tasted bitter, the coffee got cold, and she was paralysed with the question,

"What have I done?"

She lost it all in a moment of anger and frustration,

not to anybody else, but to herself. She tried to breathe, think, and speak it all, but it was too late. I had already read the letter. We never met again, she never called, and when the new school year began, she went away. That's it, I lost Michaellyn.

I was hoping against hope, waiting for an absolution that I'd never be sure would come. I wasn't so sure of what she thought of me, but I was holding on to what I believed. 'True love will return.' I would beg myself to stop dreaming of fantasies and live my life. I went to school, had fun with my friends, and studied, but when I switched off my mind at night, I thought about the memories we had together, and it haunted my beliefs and self-esteem.

Not going very often, but I loved every moment I spent at the cemetery. That is where the dead were buried, but not the feelings I had for one person-Michaellyn. Every day, I felt like I was losing myself. Since the day she left, my days and nights turned into a hellish turmoil. It didn't concern me whether my uncle's family noticed changes in me or not; I lived as though I didn't exist at all at home and in a very crowded city. I watched as the days turned into months, and the schools closed for a semester break.

Michaellyn returned to Lae from Sonoma Adventist College. And on the Sabbath day, she came to the church where she had given me the letter. I wasn't there, and she went home disappointed. She didn't want to ask anybody. The following Sabbath, she came back. She confessed there was a hollow in her soul that needed to be filled up, a love that needed rest, a soul that craved for peace and wanted to be at home.

When I saw her for the first time after eternal days of separation, my bones were cracking, and my heart wept. We hugged each other for a long time. She couldn't wait any longer to empty her heart. I listened attentively as she told me what happened when she was at college and how broken she was when she realized that she had ended our relationship.

Our eyes were constantly blinking romantically, as we were talking, maybe, to rewrite our story. At the end of the day, she confessed that she had come back for more, and we reignited and gave life to the love we thought was dead. We rewrote our stories and fell in love again, this time, more intimately. Promises are made to be broken, but she assured me that if I didn't run away, we would get married. Her raw smiles were like diamonds after the heat. We made a promise that we would get married when we finished college. That was the promise we held on to when she returned to Sonoma for another semester.

Chapter 12

Memories Before the Tragedy

I titled this chapter 'Memories Before the Tragedy' because a lot happened in this chapter. Our sweet moments quickly turned into bittersweet memories. The feeling was like a bee sting that changes the way someone looks after playing with the bee. The facial appearance would appear different. The longest phone call we've ever had. The meeting after long years of separation. The echoes of our best laughter. The longest and safest romantic walk in the city. The promises and the last goodbyes that, unknowingly, were the final ones I'd say to someone who would never return home safely.

If only I had known, I would have done this or that. Sometimes, the future is unpredictable and complicated. There were times I lost my mind reading her letters and recalling the sweet echoes of her voice. And I remind myself, is this really happening in my life, or is it just a fairy tale, a wild dream that I should give up and wake up from?

Three weeks earlier, before they closed for the year, I ignorantly called her, and we talked on the phone. It was on a Sunday, the first week of November 2010. I was told to wait a minute, as she was still working in her work line area. It's common in Adventist schools where students are introduced to a work line; it's part of the school policy. She didn't want to cut the call because of the work line. We needed to talk for a long time, so she asked me to give her a minute to round up what she was doing. The call that followed that moment was the longest call we've ever had in our entire relationship.

I couldn't tell you everything we talked about on the phone, but the nature of it was sacred and special. I felt it in my marrow and veins. I can still feel the vibration in the hand holding the phone that day. We talked about a lot of things. I remember disagreeing on most of the ideas she suggested, and we argued over some of the issues we couldn't resolve from a distance.

But I was silent when she said she'd come for the Christmas break. I never said anything about her coming to Lae, but she insisted that she should come to see her mother. Her mother had been very ill lately, and she needed her presence more than anyone else. That holiday would be special because she was going to tell her mother about our relationship.

When she came, she told me I would have to meet her family, but I suggested we could do that after she graduated. I don't want to do that. I regretted saying it because I cut her off, and she never mentioned meeting her family again, even after she came. When I ended the call, I regretted making it. I hurt her with the way I sounded on the phone. Later, she told me that she hated me more than she would have hated someone else she loved the most.

The day she arrived in Lae from East New Britain, I wasn't there. I had gone to Goroka three days earlier and never told her. She arrived and was expecting me. When she learned that I wasn't in Lae, her hopes withered, and she travelled home to Markham. She hated me for no reason, and I was worried, maybe something terrible might happen to one of us.

After I returned from the village, I travelled on a bus that was supposed to arrive in Lae in the morning (the Tulait Tulait bus, they call it). We made a stop at Young Creek, where we spent some hours. Some passengers were playing darts, smoking, and chewing betel nuts while waiting for early dawn so we could arrive in Lae in the morning.

After I arrived in Lae from Goroka, I stayed for another four days before I unexpectedly met Michaellyn. A friend of hers informed her that I had arrived in Lae a few days ago, but she never attempted to call. She must have called me, but I was out of network coverage, and I never called her either. A few days later, I followed my aunt to the market to buy fruits for her husband, who had fallen from a construction building and had been admitted to Angau Memorial Hospital. It was a ferocious accident that led to his death three months later.

At the market, we had already bought everything we needed, and on our way to the main gate, I heard a familiar voice calling gently against the chaos of noises in the area. I turned in the blink of an eye because I recognized that voice. My heart skipped a beat. No kidding, it was indeed Michaellyn, who had left her friend and hurried to where I was standing. She came and humbly gave me a hug that lasted for a couple of minutes. I was surprised. It was an unexpected meeting.

"Avu," She whispered in between, trying to catch her breath.

"Mickey."

That was all I had to say. That was all my heart

could speak when my mouth couldn't. I turned to my aunt and told her to go on ahead to the hospital, as I would follow later. She stared at me, confused, and then left us. She must have been very angry with me; I don't know. She only hurt herself with her hate. I don't care.

"Hey, you've changed a lot," she started. It had been a long time, and she had changed in appearance as well. She came from an Adventist institution and was presentable and very beautiful, more beautiful than when I last saw her. I was partly a street vendor and a student. She tied her long black hair in a single bundle and wore a shirt with the Sonoma College logo on it. In an instant, I noticed everything, every little detail of her and what she had on. The bits and pieces. Surely, I fell in love with her again.

She told me to give her a moment as she ran back to her friend, actually a mother figure. After a little conversation between them, which I could tell from a distance, Michaellyn turned and signalled me to go over to them. She must have told her friend about me, and she was smiling and nodding her head.

Her friend greeted me very warmly, introduced herself as her aunt, Mou, and was pleased to see me. I was scared at first, but seeing her smile gave me the confidence to introduce myself as well, and she allowed Michaellyn to go with me for a walk inside the marketplace, as Michaellyn had already told her. As she focused on the customers coming in, we sneaked out into the marketplace.

I was thinking of just a walk inside the marketplace and scheduling a day with Michaellyn later on. Unfortunately, it happened differently than I had anticipated. She bought some fruit at the marketplace. We went over to the other side of the road to a restaurant and bought chicken and chips. She did it all on her own accord. I never interrupted. It was only after we walked out of the restaurant that she suggested we go down to Eye Gris Market, a market by the sea.

When we got there, the place was crowded with people. We walked by the side of the boats where we sat on a flat log. The log must have been displaced by the sea. The thick clouds hid the face of the scorching sun. The sea waves crashed against our feet. A sea breeze blew, and there was peace of mind for a sweet conversation. That was before we solved the disagreements, we had on the phone a few weeks ago. Now we could talk about it when our hearts were at peace and beat in unison.

I was hungry, so I asked calmly if she could offer me something to eat. She apologized and started serving. I grabbed a pineapple from the plastic, and instead of peeling it, I just sliced it into quarters. She laughed when she noticed that the pineapple had never been peeled.

"Yu laik kaikai na go weh, na ariap,"("Where do you want to go after eating so fast") she mumbled with a curved smile. While eating, she started telling me about Sonoma and all the good things about Sonoma College. The campus and the best of all friends she had met. I decided to be a good listener that day. I never talked or interrupted. I just listened as she told me about herself and life beyond the sea of imagination.

At one point, she got up and said, "Life was fun, but you're not there, and it doesn't make any sense at all."

Maybe she was right. I don't know. There will always be friends and laughter, but the absence of someone you loved so much can make you feel like life is meaningless and not worth living. I tried to apologize for being so silly on the phone, but she cut it off, saying she forgave me right after I ended the call and was never bothered by anything I had said.

"That was the girl I loved," I said while looking at the boats lying there, and she punched me on my right arm. We resolved to meet again on Friday of that week. That was on Tuesday, so we had to wait for two more days before we could meet again. She was still in Markham and was on a return trip with her aunt to sell a bag of Marafri bananas and Kulau.

She fully expressed herself during the few moments that we had together off the shore. We missed each other, and seeing her again was all that mattered most. Her presence surely healed all the longing and burning desire I had developed over the years to see her. She was born to be mine.

We spent a few hours telling stories and watching the boats coming in and going out of the shore, carrying passengers and buai (betel nuts) bags. She told me that most of those boats travelled to and from Popondetta by night, with one floating there with an empty litter of yellow containers. It was a rare and beautiful feeling when someone you dearly loved told you something you never knew before. She was patient and never embarrassed me when I asked silly, childish questions. She treasured that moment so much, just as I did.

Back at the marketplace, her aunt was waiting eagerly for us.

"We should be leaving now; your aunt will be

waiting for us," I told her. She agreed, and we went back to the marketplace. I thanked her aunt, who was the first person in her family to know about us, and she became my best friend from then on. She offered me three bunches of Marafri bananas, bought me a coconut, and insisted that I take them. I appreciated her and took them with me to the hospital to catch up with my aunt at Angau, who was angrily waiting to talk to me. When I arrived, she was still there and accused me of taking so long.

"Tell me, you must be in love with that girl at the marketplace," she protested.

"I'm no longer sixteen, Aunty; no longer your baby boy," I exclaimed ignorantly and smiled, just to make fun and cut the topic off. I didn't want them to talk too much about Michaellyn and joke about my feelings for her because I loved that girl so much, and I was sure she loved me just as much as I loved her. We've gone through a lot, and I don't want to mess it up again.

I was expecting her on Friday, as she had told me at the beach, but she never came. She had to take her mother to the clinic. Her mother never remarried after her husband passed away. All her attention and focus were on Michaellyn, and I knew it. More than once, I recalled Michaellyn telling me about her mother. She loved Michaellyn more than anything. That Friday slipped from my hand, and I tried to find out when we could meet again. Later that day, she asked if I could be free on Monday, and we rescheduled the meeting for Monday.

There was no better place to go than the Lae War Cemetery. It had been our favourite spot since we rewrote our love stories. She came with a friend, Hariel, and we met in town. Hariel's mother was working at the Morobe Hotel in town, and when Hariel told her mother about Michaellyn, she brought them something to eat for lunch before I arrived. So, we took it with us, added on to what we bought, and headed straight to the cemetery.

Hariel was 14 years old and in grade 8. She never sat with us after lunch. She walked around by herself, collecting fallen petals and pinning them in her long-gingered hair, just like every coastal girl of her age would do to beautify their fragile body.

The place never loses its green beauty. Every time we met, the feeling was different from the previous one. The gravestones and the surrounding trees could testify to the love buried between us. They were our living witnesses. I knew Michaellyn very well. I hoped her mother and her family saw what

I saw, through the same lens I was using. She was surely raised by a gifted hand. She's very respectful, not just in the way she approached me, but in how she did certain things. Her way of thinking and the words she chooses to speak. Every time we met, in every conversation we had, she never talked badly about others, even her friends. We would only talk about what she thought about the future, and it would always be about us, not anybody else.

I realized that on that day, she had always been like that. She never talked about others, and when I started discussing people, she would turn it off respectfully. This is something more valuable she had given me, and I will always be grateful for that. There were other places within Lae City we could go, but the Lae War Cemetery is more significant and has a special place in our hearts. She preferred to sit and talk. Talk about her interests, life, future aspirations, and how her day went, whether good or bad. She had been looking for a listener. Someone who could patiently and attentively listen to her heartbeat and soul screaming.

"Namako, I think Goroka is the best place to be. After graduation, maybe we could settle in the Highlands. Safe and peaceful. I've spent the last four years of my life there, met a few friends who later became strangers, and there's one, only one, that I believe will be forever. Right here with me. Listening to every word and breath of my soul"

She finally revealed what lay buried in her heart.

"Well, that's what I've been thinking about. Living here in Lae has been a wonderful experience, but I preferred a little town, just like you do. And Goroka would be the best choice if you choose the Eastern Highlands," I replied as I picked up a fallen leaf from the lawn.

She was bothered by where we could go after graduation. A place to settle down and call home. A place to raise a family. I thought these were things of the future, but she had plans for the future. She was so good at it. She had short-term and long-term goals in life. Yes, the future is uncertain, but she didn't want to be like the common people who wake up in the morning not knowing what to do or where to go. She is not aimless about the future. I knew that because she didn't change her mind and stayed back in Lae just because of me.

She was planning to go to Sonoma, and there was nothing, not even love, that could ever intervene. I've learned a lot from Michaellyn as well. Later, I realized that she had been reading since she was a child. Michaellyn was a Kumul Bird that no longer dominated our skies. She had the mind of an eagle.

The day started to get darker, not because it was getting late, but because dark clouds were forming mountains, and we realized that we were living in a city called Rainy Lae. Just minutes before we left, she took out a book, a green-covered book from the basket she was carrying and handed it to me. I took it and fixed my eyes on the cover. It was written by an American, Dr. David Stone, on Soul Psychology. I flipped through the contents, and it was a very good book. I promised to read it and placed it nicely into my bilum. She said a friend of hers, Stella, from the Autonomous Region of Bougainville, gave it to her.

She read it and thought it would be better if I read it too. She would be spending her holiday in the village and didn't know when we would meet again, but she promised to give me a call when she came into the city. It didn't bother me; you are safe out there in the village, and you're taking good care of your mom.

We left the place and strolled down the concrete steps towards the gate. We greeted the guard as we exited the gate and headed straight to Morobe Hotel. When we reached the hotel, we realized that Hariel's mother had left already. I said goodbye and left them as she would take Hariel home.

It saddens me to realize that days and weeks are slipping by, and another year is approaching. I will walk the streets of Lae again, but someone will wave goodbye at the airport, and it will take another year to see her again. It took us years to build this relationship, and we have yet one more year to go before she finally comes home.

I believe in love that I felt was rightfully mine. A kind of love that does not ask for more, where it will always be enough. I don't know how beautiful she appeared to her family, but to me, she was enough. A Morobean will always be enough for an Eastern Highlander.

I'll continue my studies at the University of Technology, and Michaellyn will be going back to Sonoma for her final year. We have come a thousand miles, and yet not many of our families knew about us. She wants it that way, and I don't know why, but lately, she changed her mind, and I will have to meet her mother before she leaves. I repeatedly told her on several occasions that it would be inappropriate, but she wouldn't listen. Her heart was hardened.

Chapter 13

Unexpected Trip to Kabiufa

Two weeks before the 2011 academic year began, I received an anonymous call from a stranger. At first, I ignored it and let it go to voicemail, but when the phone kept ringing, I changed my mind and answered it. It was Michaellyn. She called just to let me know that she would be travelling to Goroka to see a mother in the village of Kabiufa, who had been looking after her during those years when she was a student there. I don't know why she wanted to do that. I told her not to do that, but the way she responded left me speechless and ashamed for objecting.

She offered to pay for the trip if I changed my mind to go with her. That week was going to be a very busy week for me as well, but I decided to travel with her since she would be going to my home province, and I didn't want to let her travel alone.

She came down to Lae from Markham the day before, and on Wednesday morning, we departed for Goroka. It would be another trip with Michaellyn along the Highlands Highway.

She wasn't feeling well and slept for hours. We reached Kainantu Town and dropped off some of the passengers there. While the crew was calling for a passenger to replace the ones that had gotten off, I ran to the nearby supermarket and grabbed two cans of Fanta and Sprite. I bought a Fanta for myself, but Mickey wanted a Fanta and gave me the Sprite. She hoped that we would get into Goroka Town before all the shops closed, as she intended to buy something for her mother as well.

The bus dropped us at the marketplace, and we rushed into Papindo Supermarket, where we bought something for her mother in the village before getting on a bus to Kabiufa. The mother didn't know that Michaellyn was coming to see her. I had to drop her off at home and return to town. When we got there, we were told by her neighbours that she was away for a house cry at Asaroka and would be home soon. We sat on the nicely cut lawn and waited until dusk, and I was already late getting back to town.

Michaellyn was afraid that her Kabiufa mother would spend the night at the *haus krai*, but the kind neighbours assured us that she would still come home. Seeing that she took so long, the neighbours took us into their home and offered us dinner. We told them about the visit, and they were impressed. Most of them confessed that they recognized Michaellyn, but it had been years, and she had grown up with a slight change in her physical appearance.

Not long after, the mother came. She couldn't recognize Michaellyn either, as it was dark. Michaellyn had to explain to her that she was the one she used to call "Pikinini blo mi" (My child) some years ago, when she was a student there. The mother recalled and cried, *"Aiyo pikinini blo mi!"* and hugged her tightly, never letting her go. Her husband had passed away a year ago, and Michaellyn hadn't known about it. She was very sorry when she talked about the tragedy. The mother quickly lit the fire and peeled the kaukau. I took the peeler from her hand and peeled the remaining kaukau while the mother went out and harvested sako leaves (greens) from her garden with a torch. We boiled the rice and cooked the sako leaves with the tinned fish and noodles we had bought at the supermarket.

The mother had two daughters who were married, and she was living with her two granddaughters, who were attending Kuso Adventist Primary School.

We told many stories. There were many left unsaid, as it was getting late, and the mother was tired. Very early in the morning, she made us a delicious breakfast and tea.

When she learned that we would be leaving in the morning, she urged us to stay another day with her in the village. Michaellyn agreed, and we stayed one more day. She took us to her mountainside garden. The familiar footpaths, where we could see our old footprints, were the tracks we usually followed when hiking up the mountains. We reached the garden, and the taro was ready for harvest. We watched as she harvested enough to take with us to Lae. She dug some for us to have for dinner in the evening as well.

We let the mother prepare them for us, and we carried them home. The mother was so kind to us. Not only to us, but I believe she had been good to other students who passed through Kabiufa High School as well. She was truly blessed to be a blessing to others.

Very early in the morning, she helped us to the bus stop in town, and we got on the bus to Lae. Michaellyn promised her that she would return after graduation. I could see tears of joy forming in her eyes, between her smiles, as she waved at us when the bus left the bus stop and turned onto the highway.

Michaellyn was satisfied that one of the tasks on her to-do list, to visit a mother at Kabiufa was ticked off.

"I don't know if I'll come back to find her still alive," she said to herself while leaning against the half-opened window. I assured her that she was healthy and would be alright, as she worked in her garden and ate from what it produced.

"I hope so," she mumbled and looked out of the window toward Markham Plain as we zigzagged down the Kassam Pass.

As the cold wind displaced the hot air in the bus, it carried the feeling along the Markham Valley, flowing away. A thought crossed her mind, and she turned to me and said something that crushed my heart.

"Avundigi, have you realized that this time next year, we will be living together?"

I wasn't expecting that. I turned and looked right into her eyes. She was not kidding; she was serious and confident in what she was saying. I went silent for a while and smiled, thinking about what life would be like after getting married and hoping for a better family. From that moment on, our hearts beat in unison. We were not the only ones on the bus.

There were other passengers as well. There were children on their mother's laps, young people, and those with grey hair. They all had their own stories to tell as we travelled on.

"What if we met with an accident and one of us passed away?" I joked.

Michaellyn turned and firmly told me to shut up. I regretted saying it. Those sitting in front of us turned and tried to see what had happened behind, for she was loud. How foolish I was then. She couldn't imagine the pain of losing someone she loved. Sometimes, we say things so foolishly without considering the consequences. I felt the sting of it and almost ruined the whole trip.

We stopped at 10 Mile to repair a flat tire. After that, we travelled smoothly down to the great city of Lae. The day we travelled was Friday, and I was already exhausted. Michaellyn was also tired. We were supposed to get off at Eriku, where most of the passengers got off, but the crew, a nice guy and a friend from Asaro, told the driver that we had some passengers with a bag of taro from Kamkumung and Tent City. He then drove me to Awagasi and brought Michaellyn to Ten City late. My uncle was there waiting for me when I got off, and he carried the bag of taro home.

Since it was Friday and we were late, we left everything as it was, ate what they had prepared, and rested for the night. I never enjoyed the creamed chicken because my stomach was upset that day due to the long, tiring trip. It was easy to go to bed at night, but it was difficult for me to ignore the thoughts creeping into my mind about missing Michaellyn as the days of her departure slowly approached. There were twists and turns until daybreak. Very early in the morning, I took a bath and was ready for church when others woke up. I didn't want to talk to anyone. I didn't want to be disturbed.

I watched through the window, and as soon as I saw the bright rays of the morning sun shining through the coconut leaves, I went out and sat on the tires that were used as a flower bed wall, with the book Michaellyn had given me. I was supposed to read, but I got stuck on the photo inside and stared at it until it was time for me to go to church.

I switched off my old Nokia phone and didn't call anyone, including Michaellyn, for the next few days. My uncle was a very playful man. Everyone loved to be around him because he joked a lot. When we were at church, he took the book Michaellyn gave me, the green one about Soul Psychology, and flipped through the pages with photos of Michaellyn inside.

He poked my side and smiled. I ignored him and concentrated until the worship service ended and we came back home.

"Son, you've got a nice girl, an angel. Where is she from?" he asked as we entered the gate. Talk about love, but when you mentioned Michaellyn, you already pierced my soul.

"She is beautiful, a beautiful one from Finschhafen... I meant Markham," I replied. We spent a moment talking about girls, how he first met his wife, and so on, while waiting for lunch to be served. After I filled my tummy, I went to bed, never to be disturbed by anyone again.

The same fever caught Michaellyn, and she didn't want to talk to me either. She tried to eat, but the food tasted bitter to her. It's our thoughts that create our reality, and sometimes, they destroy us. She was torturing herself with her own thousand thoughts. She travelled to Markham on Sunday and stayed there for the next three days. She met with her friends, talked to each one personally, and was satisfied. They made a family feast in her honour, and they all celebrated. She would be away for another year, and some said their farewells with tears. She was the first and only one in their family to go to college and would be graduating the following year.

She took her mother with her on the way back to Lae. Her mother was to stay with Michaellyn until she got on the plane to Sonoma the following week. I truly believe, with no doubt in my heart, that during those few days they were together, they were treasured by Michaellyn as much as they were by her mother.

I was right. I never intervened either. Michaellyn took her mother wherever she thought best, places her mother would love. She bought her the best food and the best dress. She did everything that would bring a smile and happiness to her mother's heart. She loved hearing her voice when she talked to her. And finally, she had to do one last thing, introduce her mother to me. I said we'd do that next year, but she hardened her heart and wanted it now. I still don't know the reason why.

Chapter 14

Meeting her Family

For reasons unknown to me, I was about to meet her mother.

"No! Not today!"I told Michaellyn, "you're still studying, I am still studying, let's not do this."

Yet it was very difficult for me to convince her to postpone the meeting to the next or the following year. After an intense argument, I resolved to meet her mother. I had heard her stories, seen her photos, and now I would have to meet her in person. That was the most honourable thing I could do, Michaellyn said. I was ready to meet her. I had so much respect for her. She would become my mother as well once the knot was tied.

I had this controversial feeling about what her mother might think of me. How would she react when she sees me? Would I be accepted? I could love Michaellyn, that happened naturally, but her mother held all the blessings in the palm of her hands. I knew that very well. My mother also holds my marriage blessings in her hands.

Michaellyn needed to meet my mother as well. We'd decided it would be after she returned from Sonoma, but now it was my turn to meet her mother. Michaellyn suggested we meet somewhere in town, but I didn't want to do that. I made up my mind to go home, to where she was staying. I didn't care where that was. I would take any risk involved; I told Michaellyn. She agreed, but she would have to talk to her uncle, David, since she was staying with him. There is no other right place than where your mother is living. She took my words seriously and decided to talk to her uncle David.

When Michaellyn told him about it, he burned with anger.

"Are you crazy, Michaellyn, you're still a student?" he told her. Michaellyn knew she was in trouble. David did not know that Akaliah and Michaellyn had already resolved the issue. But David was disappointed.

"No! You're not bringing anybody here."

Michaellyn sat quietly, without a word. Then

Akaliah got up and explained to David what Michaellyn told her.

"So, you and your daughter talked about a boy who is in love with Michaellyn, on the street, and now you want to convince me to accept him?" David stood up aggressively and told Akaliah in the face and walked out.

He stood on the veranda for a while and returned. When he came in, he apologised to Michaellyn and asked her to tell a little bit about him, and the relationship we had. After Michaellyn told him vividly, he changed his mind and said it's okay to meet us for a friendly chat. That would happen on Sunday when he would be at home. I never told my uncle, with whom I lived, about my plans. I never revealed the risk I was about to take to anyone in my family.

Michaellyn told her mother and David everything she knew about me before I came. She knew me better than I knew myself. David was positive, after the argument, and so was her mother. These two were very important to me. I didn't mind what anyone else thought. Michaellyn also explained to them why it was important for them to meet me. I was getting nervous as the daylight turned into evening shadows.

I couldn't recall the exact time, but it was around 10 a.m. I went alone to see her mother and her uncle's family. Along the way, I was troubled. What would I say? I had prepared my words, but I wasn't sure if they were the right ones. I drove all my fears away and headed straight to their house, not far from the bus stop at Tent City.

At the bus stop, Michaellyn tried to talk to me like she usually did, but her throat was blocked, and tears formed in her eyes. I was emotional as well. Just a glance from a classroom window had led me to ask for her mother's blessing to tie the knot for life with Michaellyn. It was a little bit complicated.

David welcomed me at the gate of his residence, and I felt welcome. Her mother was inside the house with a few others, including David's wife and children. I felt truly welcome when the owner of the house greeted me at the gate. He was a true Morobean. I was given a seat close to her mother. Michaellyn sat on the other side of the table with David.

As David started to speak, there was silence in the room. He welcomed me again in front of everyone and allowed Michaellyn to tell them about us. That was the opportunity she had been waiting and praying for. She shared how, from just being friends, we turned our relationship into something more, how it happened and where.

She told them how long we'd been together and what we were anticipating in the coming years. She also mentioned that it was important for her to introduce me to them before she left. And finally, she had to confess that I was the reason why she went to Okapa right after the National Examination. David made a brief remark in response to what Michaellyn had said and then told me a little about Michaellyn. He shared things I already knew. Then, he allowed me to speak.

I began by introducing myself. Everyone listened attentively. Her mother rested her palm on her cheeks and paid close attention as I spoke about their daughter. I never talk much about myself. I simply mentioned my name and where I come from, then I began talking about Michaellyn. I was surprised to find that they knew so little about her. I could start from her birth, I knew it, but it felt inappropriate to do so. So, I began from where I was supposed to, where I met her.

As I dug deeper into who Michaellyn is to me, her mother lowered her head. She knew who her daughter was, but she had no idea about the struggles and dark places Michaellyn had fought so hard to overcome. I told them about the good I knew of her, how blessed her parents should feel, and how thankful they should be for raising someone with such a down-to-earth attitude. Michaellyn lowered her head as well.

She probably thought I hadn't noticed those little attributes she possessed. She was pleased. It didn't take long for me to say everything that was on my mind. Her mother took my hand and held it firmly for a while before saying, "Thank you."

I stayed longer than expected. They served delicious food, and we ate, shared other stories, and chatted until it was time for me to go home. Akaliah and Michaellyn walked me to the roadside. I gave Akaliah a final hug and exited the gate and Michaellyn said, "Hey, I never expected you to say what you said. You always have something sweet and heartwarming to say."

"I just couldn't let this opportunity slip by," I replied. "I needed to tell them who you are to me. But I appreciate it. I wouldn't have done it if you hadn't arranged it. Finally, I'm free".

The rare feeling of acceptance was still there when she said goodbye and returned home. I didn't turn back; I walked to the bus stop and headed home.

Chapter 15

Final Day with Michaellyn

When you love someone, truly love them, a part of
you is divided. It's a game of roses versus thorns.
It's a war—not with anyone else, but with yourself,
your soul, and your mind. I fell into that trap, and
the rest is history now.

The day was drawing near. She'd be leaving soon. I had just met her mother and her uncle, and they'd agreed. The puzzled thoughts in my mind began to unfold as I rested my head on my pillow in the middle of the night, staring at the fan spinning on the ceiling. I was drawn to that girl. It's easy to dream about her along the way.

She'd be leaving on Monday. The registration would begin that week, starting on Monday. I was prepared for another academic year and was positive about life. But there was a strange feeling, like a cloud hovering above my head. I had never felt it before. We were supposed to spend the last Sabbath at her church, but it didn't happen for reasons she kept from me. However, on the last Sunday, we decided to tour the University of Technology campus.

I didn't need to explain everything about the campus to her; she already knew. We arrived at one of the classroom buildings, which belonged to the Engineering Department. It was a nice place.

There were no dark clouds in the sky, only scattered ones. She was wearing a blue T-shirt that day and had her favourite string bilum, which her mother had recently given her, over her shoulder. She looked so beautiful on that sunny Sunday under the shade of a large tree. There was nothing left for us to talk about. She looked at the dried leaves scattered on the neatly cut lawn, then at me. I turned toward her and realised that she was also looking at me. I lifted my head and caught her eyes fixed on mine. She smiled, and I smiled back. I had once fallen in love with that smile years ago in high school.

"You're killing me with your smile. You always do," I complimented her. It was an honest compliment from a sincere, yet visible admirer. She looked away and tried to snatch the umbrella from my hand. She took it, and I'm sure she kept it with her.

"Mickey," I said, as that was how I pronounced her name. She looked at me, expecting me to say something, anything at all.

"I just want you to know that whatever happens, during the few months you'll be away, I will be here, loving you—only you. We've come a long way, and we're still here, facing each other because we believe in love. We knew it was ours. You'll always be first. You'll always be mine. And now, nothing, absolutely nothing, could stop me from keeping you. I can lose half of me, even all of me, just for you. You've saved me from myself."

"Namako," she replied. It was her favourite word. It simply means "lewa" in my Okapa Fore Tok Ples. "You always told me you loved me. And I believe in what you said. Namako, I just want to be with you forever, for the rest of my life."

We sat there, talking in a low, sad tone of voice. She was there, right in front of me, talking to me, and I missed her already. I had hours left, slipping away in the blink of an eye. She told me that whenever I missed her, I should come here, sit in the same place we sat, and read the book she gave me. She would be found in the poems, letters, and books she gave me. She always wanted me to read. She had this habit of buying books from the bookstore and second-hand shops, so I could read.

"I want you to have this. Please keep it until I come back. My mother will be worried, but I'm not going to tell her it will be with you. She gave it to me with all her heart. It's so special. You're more special, and I want you to carry it on Sabbaths."

"I'll imagine you carrying it to church. I'll always be proud. I'll come back for you. You'll be in my heart for the time I'm away,"

She said all this without looking at me. She removed her Morobe string bilum from her side and gave it to me. Inside, there were two biros, one black and one blue, and a light green-covered book, her favourite, written by Elizabeth Elliot and titled Quest of Love.

Later, I discovered it featured many distant love stories. I loved reading them all. It was at that moment I understood why it was written in the book of Genesis that a man shall leave his father and mother and be united to his wife, and they will become one flesh.

Michaellyn and I were already one in heart. I took

the bilum, looked at it again and again, and tried to carry it the Goroka way, across my shoulder. It fitted perfectly. She looked at it and was greatly satisfied. I took it out again and wore it in front of me like a Morobean kid. It looked even better now, because the handle was made to be worn that way. We stood up and were about to leave the campus. It was like a thick darkness had swept over my face, even though the sun was still overhead. Saying goodbye to someone I dearly loved.

We walked to the bus stop, and when she disappeared, I was left alone like a lost animal wandering around the campus, just waiting for the pain in my heart to die down so I could go home. I didn't follow her onto the bus. She left alone.

"That was the last time I saw her and received her last warm hug".

She got on the bus and was never to be seen again. I assured myself it would be okay. I stayed back on campus until nearly 6 pm and then went home. I didn't talk to her again until she got settled on campus.

On Monday, while it was still dark outside, she woke up and began writing poems. A poem a day heals the distant feeling of missing. Writing poems truly heals. She promised herself that she would write a poem every single day until she returned.

The first poem she wrote was titled "Let Me Love You." I was impressed when I read it as a text a few months later.

When the daylight broke through the dark, Michaellyn, Lulume, and her mother left for the airport at Nadzab. Her aunt must have been with them, but I have no idea. Her mother had been with her throughout the holiday. Michaellyn promised her mother that she would return at the end of the year and that she shouldn't worry so much about her. When the plane arrived, Michaellyn hugged her mother and Lulume and they cried openly. Her mother cried too, burying her daughter in her arms and wept. The scene was so emotional. Others were there too, families leaving their sons and daughters who were going to schools in Port Moresby and other parts of the Southern Region.

They made a boarding call, and Michaellyn grabbed her bag and left. Her mother watched until she was out of sight. That was it; she was gone. Little did she know that Michaellyn was leaving forever. Surely, we live in a cruel world where life is unfair and sometimes unpredictable. Michaellyn transited through Port Moresby and then flew to Tokua Airport, heading to Sonoma Adventist College.

Her mother wiped her tears away so she could watch the plane take off, disappearing into the thick clouds, which looked like the long-range mountains. A broken-hearted mother left Nadzab Airport that day. Michaellyn had asked me to do one simple thing for her, her only favour, and that was to meet her mother and have a moment to chat with her whenever she came down to Lae. Her mother went home and never returned, never to be seen again. Loneliness is indeed a very selfish thing. No one teaches you how to do it properly, so you make up your own rules and carry on.

PART THREE

MV Rabaul Queen

The MV Rabaul Queen Tragedy

It's a long, lonely story, as I recollect the memories.

Stories of great love and invisible magic.

Stories of Dark Mysteries, unprecedented tragedies, and hopelessness. Stories of a feeling that has never been fully expressed.

A journey of a Young Lover that ended halfway.

Final Goodbyes from the other side of the ocean were never heard, sweet kisses that were too salty for the soul. Hands that were too cold from the midnight waters.

A Lily of the Lonely Valley in Morobe Province.

An elegant smile that was engulfed by the angry waves. A shipwreck that claimed the lives of many. Love that was buried alive in the night's dawn. A world that was so loud to hear their agonizing cries.

Yet, many were never found. Only the skies and the highest heavens have listened to and recorded how many souls were lost to history in that fateful tragedy.

Dark clouds have hidden the face of February's moonlight. All the stars must have fallen, for it was dark as in the graves.

You're almost home, my love, my forever fervent one.

It didn't come to mind that, miles away,

my heart has been waiting eagerly to collide with yours and beat as one forever, in unison.

Your life was an unprecedented tragedy.

I've been waiting for daybreak, which has happened in Paradise.

My life is a Dark Mystery, I'll be waiting for you forever by the sandless beaches of Morobe Province.

My beautiful one with a String Bilum around her neck.

Arise and come to me, my dove-like love, with kisses so tender and sweet as wild honey.

My heart will always be in pain,

The loss I can't regain.

Chapter 16

Onboard the MV Rabaul Queen

December 25, 2011

"Hey!"

"Hello, good morning. Forgive me for calling you in the early hours of the morning. I just want to tell you something, it shouldn't be long, can I?"

"You're good to go, girl."

"Hey, I hope to see you soon. I can't wait, love you."

"Hahaha, you're so funny. I love you, too."

"Don't you forget, this year is ours?"

"I have bundles of roses already in bloom."

"Hope to see you soon, very soon."

"I'll be wai...waiting for you......"

The call ended.

Two weeks earlier, my uncle asked me if I would go home for a Christmas break in the village. I was determined to go home too, but the expectation that Michaellyn would come very soon kept me back in Lae. And now, I was home alone. Everyone had gone, and I was lonely as the sea. But my heart went cold when she told me she was not coming during Christmas.

I was worried. But my greatest fear was, what if the food ran out, and I had nothing to keep me going for the next few weeks while my uncle was away? There was enough rice in the bucket, a pack of tinned fish in the cupboard, and enough flour. I was the only one at home, and that is enough for me.

Although Michaellyn had a wonderful holiday back in Rabaul with so much to be thankful for, she still paused to think about us and where we would have been for Christmas if she were here. Michaellyn and her friend would be coming to Lae together, and I was already losing patience.

I can't wait any longer. Hoping, praying, and wishing that the days should slip off quickly, and they'd be here. Finally, the short holiday ended, and they left Sonoma in the dull weather and travelled to Rabaul Town on Monday. They got their tickets ready on Tuesday for a trip with the MV Rabaul

Queen. The ferry was on its way to Rabaul from the Autonomous Region of Bougainville.

MV Rabaul Queen anchored in Rabaul Main Wharf at approximately 06:25 am on 1st February. After the ship took fuel and water, the passengers boarded, including Michaellyn and her friend. It would be an overnight trip to Kimbe, then to Lae. I was expecting Michaellyn early Thursday. She did tell me that I should meet her at the Wharf if I had nothing to do that day. I was very excited and told her, "I'll be waiting for you. Make sure to come home safely."

They arrived in Kimbe at around 11 a.m. At the main wharf, she made another call, and we talked and joked and laughed while they were waiting for the ship. She asked if the weather here in Lae was appealing, for it was raining and dull at her end. She told me her mother is in Lae and will also be at the Wharf waiting. I told her I'd find her when I got there. She didn't want to buy any food, except some packets of chicken-flavoured Snax and a few cans of pineapple-flavoured Fanta. She was not good at eating on the ship because of past experiences.

When she got onboard, she realized that the ship was overcrowded. There were a lot of people, more crowded than when they left Rabaul. Many decided to stay back. A mother with three children, who was there with Michaellyn, changed her mind and stayed back, but her friend insisted that they should continue. I did tell her to stay back and come on a plane, but her friend hardened her heart, for she had a lot to do in Lae in the coming days. She was among many students and teachers, for the 2012 academic year had just begun. There were mothers with their babies, young men and women, and children. It was another casual day for another journey out to the sea.

They left Kimbe Wharf around 4 pm and set sail towards Cape Campbell. There, the ship faced the prevailing, strong easterly wind. There were more passengers, though the vessel was certified to carry 295 passengers. It was so crowded that mothers with babies and children couldn't sleep or sit well. It was packed and overloaded. Michaellyn was sitting on the Starboard Deck. As they continued on the voyage and travelling through the Vitiaz Strait, the rough conditions at sea increased, and the rain began to fall heavily on them, and they moved over to the port side, which is positioned above the upper deck. As more people moved to port side, they exerted more weight on that side.

A few moments later, I called again, but I couldn't reach them. They must have been out of the network coverage area. They were fighting against the waves and storms. After several missed calls, her friend answered the call and gave the phone to Michaellyn. From the tone of her voice I could tell that they were in danger. She spoke as fast as she could, and I couldn't hear most of the words she was saying. All I could hear was, "Namako, I'll call you back later, after the storm," and the call ended.

It was very late in the middle of the night. I threw the phone on the side of the bed and went to sleep.

While I was sound asleep,

While I was dreaming of the roses,

While I was sleeping peacefully,

Resting comfortably under my blanket,

Resting my head on cozy pillows,

When the night was so sweet with memories,

My only love was aggressively attacked by terrible storms and angry winds.

She became very scared and afraid when the spray from the sea continued to attack the starboard deck, where she was staying. The situation grew worse, and she moved into an indoor accommodation. Because many souls were moving to another deck, the vessel leaned to the other side. The starboard quarters were hit by large waves, and the upper deck began taking in more water. Many people became confused as the ship was in a critical condition. They didn't know what to do. Some were afraid and tried to find a safe place and life jackets. Some smart ones were calling out to the angry waves jokingly, "One more, one more," when the ship was leaning on one side. They never realized the danger ahead of them.

2nd February 2012

At around 05:45 am they could see the Morobe coastline. The place became clearer. In my twists and turns in the early hours of dawn, the ship was attacked by three large waves on the starboard side, and the port side became submerged in the water. The waters started rushing into the accommodation side when the second wave hit the starboard side.

I was in a deep sleep, the kind you don't want to be disturbed from, when the third wave hit the hull and the ship capsized. Those who had been travelling on the ship for years or had experienced it before, or had been told by others, jumped into the waters and started swimming a few minutes before the ship sank.

As soon as the ship submerged itself into the waters, oil and fuel began floating on the surface, and the sea became black. Life rafts and boats were not enough for everyone. By then, most of the babies were seen floating on the surface, dead. Their mothers must have kissed them goodbye praying as they let go of their little hands. How terrible it was to know the end from the very beginning! No one could hear anyone. Everyone was screaming, crying, shouting, and praying at the top of their voices. The waves of the sea turned black because of the fuel and oil. The waves continued to roar, making it difficult for some to swim.

Where was Michaellyn at that time?

The rescue team was on its way, alerted by the Australian Maritime Safety Authority. Helicopters and other ships with several boats were involved in the search, but the wind and the waves made the rescue very difficult, almost impossible. MOL Summer was the first vessel to arrive at the scene and rescued 116 survivors. All the survivors were transferred to the Lae Harbour Tug boat Victory and transported to Lae.

It was the eternal end of a 20-hour journey; it was the end of the Rabaul Queen at approximately 06:00am. Various sources testified that more than 246 souls were rescued. Those who were badly injured were transported to Angau Memorial Hospital in

Lae. Some couldn't save themselves. Death claimed more lives in less than 10 minutes when the ship went down slowly in up to 3000 meters of water, to her eternal destiny.

The Rabaul Queen now rests peacefully at the bottom of the Solomon Sea.

Michaellyn was never found.

Chapter 17

The Search

When I woke up in the morning, it was already 6:45am. I knew I was late, so I decided to leave without breakfast. I was hurrying to the main road when I heard the news of a sinking vessel. Everyone was talking about the Rabaul Queen. My heart started beating vigorously. I was too scared to make a phone call or ask anyone to confirm if it was the MV Rabaul Queen that brought Michaellyn. As I rushed up to Awagasi Market, I confirmed that it was true. I lost my way to the wharf. My life has never been the same.

What happened to Michaellyn?

She must have passed away along with many others, and her body would never be recovered.

After searching relentlessly for days, hoping against hope, I prayed for a chance to see her face, even if she was found dead. Just to have a grave to call her eternal home. But when I found nothing, I was completely traumatized and heartbroken. I lost my appetite. I couldn't think straight. I couldn't make decisions right. I couldn't visit the places I once loved. I lost sleep, and my eyes turned red from exhaustion.

A million questions hibernate in my mind, breaking my heart. Why did this happen to me? Of all the billions of people in the world, why did this life's tragedy choose me? I blame myself for everything that went wrong. I tried to understand, but I failed. I do not know what her last thought was, what she was thinking when the ship started to sink into the depths of the darkest sea. She must have thought of me, for she knew I was waiting, or her mother. She must have fought against the pressure and the currents — aiyo, no yah, namako nene. She did see the Morobe coastline, but what happened to her?

I believe even the angels watched with their hands behind their backs, the struggle she was going through. I believe many held onto hope with every last breath. In fact, there were survivors. Many were reunited with their families and loved ones. But why was my love never found, dead or alive? She must have been carried by the waves to a place where I can only imagine. A place that now exists only in the corners of my mind. She must have waited long enough for dawn's deliverance. This, I do not know. Only heaven knows. It's a sad mystery now. I have accepted the love that I believe is mine. I know, without a doubt, that she did the same. We believed in our bright future.

Life is complicated and unpredictable.

My love for Michaellyn is the kind of love I don't have to fight for. It's mine, and it will always be mine. There is no compromise, no inch of doubt. People say that time heals all wounds, but to me, that is a myth. Time never really heals. As days turned into months and years, I found myself lost in a world of, "Mickey, if only you were here, we should have been this and that", or "I remember the first day I met you. You wore the best smile that day, and I hit the classroom wall with my fist. I never even felt the pain"

I kept knocking, but you never answered. I slept, but my mind was awake. Between us now lies a deep ocean, Mickey. Those who survived were given a second chance at life. They have their own stories to tell. But the page of my life where your story belongs will remain blank, black, and empty. Forever is a long, long time, Honey.

Wherever you may be, I just want you to know that I tried relentlessly to find you, from home to the wharf, from the hospital where survivors and bodies were brought in, and back to the shore. But I was left waiting. For the first few days after the sinking, I wished someone would call me or meet me and say, "She's here" or "We found her body," but you were never found.

I don't even know where I found the strength to keep searching, but I did it anyway, because I had to find you. My world fell apart and was crushing me, and I didn't have the strength to stand. I still have your photos in my album, your handwritten letters, and your Sonoma College logo shirt. I kept them but haven't looked at them in a long time. Those precious memories felt like a prison since we parted ways.

Every boat that arrived, every rescue team that came, I ran towards them, hoping to find you. There was no one to lean on, no one to run to when the waves of shattered dreams crashed against me. I fought it alone because I believed in us, in our love, in our future, in our happily ever after. A few days later, I sat by the shore, lonely and hopeless. This was not a dream where I could wake up and escape reality. The ocean pretended to be calm, as if it hadn't just buried my love days ago. We came a long way, and you knew it well. You were my almost-home—almost. If only we could go back in time and relive the life we have left behind, maybe the story would have been different.

I stood among others looking for their loved ones. Mothers who lost their sons and daughters. Husbands who lost their wives and children. Students who were on their way to school in the highlands. Many of them were among the passengers who were never found. The pain ran deep, cutting through me like a knife. We shared sorrow, though words could never express the depth of our loss. The fortunate ones were reunited with their families. But I waited in vain. You were gone without footprints, without a trace. How could I find you?

Tell me, how can I love you, even in death?

PART FOUR

Lonely Hearts

Chapter 18

Unsent Letter to Michaellyn

My heart almost stopped beating. My mind went blank, and I was about to sleep when ten-year-old Kisiwa ran into the room and screamed my name,

"Avundigi, someone is here to see you! She's at the gate!"

The message took too long to reach my conscious mind. When I finally came outside, the gate was open. The visitor was unfamiliar to those in the house, so she stood outside respectfully. It was Delphine.

When she saw me, she met me halfway and cried loudly by burying me in her arms. I couldn't hold back anymore. I cried openly. We stood there for a long time. Everyone was confused. They know nothing about Michaellyn, except my uncle, but he didn't know where she was or what happened to her. I invited her inside. She was the one who told my uncle's family everything about Michaellyn and me, how our love began and how it had ended in tragedy.

My uncle's wife, from Salamoa, who had lost her father at sea, broke down in tears and cried bitterly. The children cried too. They shared my sorrow, unknowingly saving me from my loneliness. Others had tried to comfort me, Delphine, Lindon, and a few others, but the pain still clung to me, like a thorn buried deep in my soul.

Tragedy is an evil thing. We can do nothing to change it. It comes in whatever form it wants, whenever it chooses. Some days, I laugh. I joke with friends. I pretend I have moved on. But when she crosses my mind, it cuts me down the middle and leaves me falling apart in different directions. I believe there is hope, somewhere, and I'm going to find it with all my mind, heart and soul. For now, let me stitch my wounded heart with unsent letters, just to stop the bleeding. But where do broken hearts go anyway, when the healing seems a long and lonely process!?

Dear Michaellyn | phyphy

Those naysayers, pretenders of life realities, told me to move on, to accept what had happened between us, and urged me to live a simple life so that no one could pass judgment on me. But I just want you to know that I still loved you, silently. Just like how the moon loves the night. Like how the stars love the night sky. I hope, every day and night, that one day I'll meet you when the sun kisses the ocean, and the moon kisses the mountains. My heart is longing for you, heavy with pain and so many memories of losing you. I'm keeping you, honey, so close to my heart, like honey glued to the honeycomb.

Chapter 19

I don't know how to move on!

[In Poetic Verse]

Two Years Later, I still grieve over the girl I love endlessly and lost eternally in the sinking of the Passenger Ferry MV Rabaul Queen. In my own way, I tried to separate the past from the present. I tried to heal, to move on, to accept life's harsh treatment by taking away my future, my hope, and to be happy, at least for a minute. But I couldn't, for everything I thought I knew about life, love, and the future with Michaellyn had shattered and drowned in the sea two years ago.

The pain, the grief, the loneliness, and the intense isolation are still here, clinging to me, so irresistible. How could I possibly have lost it all in a minute, and woke up in the morning to realise that what we've built over the years has gone? Honestly, my heart was like an open wound that had never been really healed. Losing Michaellyn in such a harsh way is something I truly couldn't escape. She came from nowhere, painted my life with all the colours of love, and disappeared. Now, I don't know what to do.

I went back home, trying to run away from the memories. I avoided people I think who might remind me of her, but her footprints still remain, even at the door of my isolated house in the valley of Purosa. I never told my parents that the girl who came here some years ago with Hannah was my girlfriend, and that she passed away when the ferry sank. But they could read the subtitles in a way that I act, talk, and do certain things.

I thought going home, far from the shores could help, but no matter how far I went, no matter how many miles I distanced myself from the ocean that buried Michaellyn alive, the memories of her were always there, glued to my flesh and bones, like shadows that refused to leave, even on sunny days. I never talked about it to Lindon, Hannah, Delphine, and a few others whom Mickey and I crossed paths with, though each of them shares the heavy weight of the pain I felt.

One day, I decided to travel back to Lae. I sat in the back seat of a bus when travelling. I opened the window just to let the cool air in as the bus left

Goroka Town and accelerated down to Kainantu. I never ate and never bothered talking to anyone on the bus. On that journey, I could still hear her voice; I could feel her presence by my side because we once travelled together many times on that road. No one on the bus knew I was grieving over my lost love. And it doesn't matter anymore, loneliness is indeed a selfish thing, and it's my share of it.

When we arrived at the Umi Market in Markham Valley, I knew I had come to her place. I don't want to go out of the bus and retrace or erase her footprints, or meet any of her relatives. I just don't want to share the pain. I wanted to feel it selfishly. Because, for me, that place felt empty, like the world was moving around me while I sat still, stuck in a moment that I couldn't escape.

After everyone got off the bus, something of nature forced me and I got out of the bus. I didn't care or know where I was going, but I was moving my feet into the market place. I bought roasted peanuts, and without eating them, I leaned against the fence for a minute before going back to get a Kulau.

On my way into the marketplace, I saw a woman who was already looking at me. She looked familiar. We haven't met since the day we got the news of the sinking vessel. She, too, had been swallowed by the grief that day, as I was, and somehow, she'd disappeared from my life, just like Michaellyn had. She wasn't a person I ever expected to cross paths with again, certainly not in a place like this. I was shocked to see her selling roasted peanuts and kulau. When our eyes met, I could see the same pain in her eyes that I felt in mine. I knew losing a child was a pain that was too big to comprehend. It creates a hole in the heart that nothing can fill.

She didn't speak at first. She just stared at me, like she wasn't sure if I was real or if she was imagining me in this crowded market. When I moved closer to her, she could tell clearly that I was the one. Then, without warning, her face turned pale, and her tears started falling. It was as though the last year of her life, all the moments she had tried to hold together, all the times she had pushed the grief down, had finally caught up with her, and she sobbed in front of me. And, at that moment, I couldn't stop my tears as well.

She stood up from where she was and came to me. She had lost so much weight, her eyes became weak, and her health was also falling. She was not the woman I knew. She approached me and, without a word, took refuge in my arms and sobbed silently. Her tears fell uncontrollably, so hard as if to dig a ditch in the hardest soil. No one could hear the sound of her grieving. I never said a word. Even if I wanted to, I didn't know what the right words to use would be, and so I gave her a sacred moment to fully express her emotions. She looked up at me and said,

"Son, I can't let her go".

She'd been honest, I can tell it.

"I can't forget her".

"How could you forget a child?"

"How could you move on from something like this?"

I didn't have an answer. I still didn't have an answer a year later. How could I? What could anyone say to a mother who had lost her child in such a violent, senseless, and tragic way? Words felt like empty promises. Like they would shatter the moment they were spoken.

We stood there and chatted for a while. She told me how she looked for her that day, too. I also did the same. We shared every memory we had with Michaellyn. I took out the string bilum from my bag. The same bilum she gave to her daughter Michaellyn, and she gave me at the University of Technology. Then I honestly confess to Akaliah,

"I don't know how to move on, to be myself again. It feels like she's still here, doesn't it? Like any minute now, I'll hear her voice again, or she'll walk through the market stalls, calling out to me. But she's not coming back. And I don't know how to deal with that."

She mentioned me to wait, as she returns back to collect her belongs. Most of her sales items has been sold, and those that remained, she told a friend to take care of it. I got my bag from the bus, and she took me home. As we were conversing alone the way, she sounded like Michaellyn and I heard her voice in her mother's tone. We came and stood on that bridge, and she said,

"I am a mother, and my heart is totally broken. I will never stop loving my daughter Michaellyn. She was my only daughter, my hope, my only one".

I thought I was the only person who loved and lost Michaellyn, but her mother showed me a scar that would never be healed.

Many have crossed the bridge, but we're still here, grieving over the loss, because we don't know how to move on.

Many stories will never be told, but it will be buried in the hearts forever.

"Nasonamako,
I never visited the Lae War Cemetery
Since the day you were gone till now,
And never will I in the future".

Naso~Namako,
May your Soul rest in Eternal Peace
"My heart will always be in deep pain
of losing you".

Michaellyn Denevi
October 01, 1987 — February 02, 2012

nasonamako poetry_naso caleb kila